Somewhere In Time

José F. Nodar

Camden Books Publishing

Somewhere in Time / José F. Nodar
ISBN: 978-1-7643714-2-1 Paperback
ISBN: 978-1-7643714-3-8 E-Book
ISBN: 978-1-7643714-4-5 Audiobook

Dedication

In loving memory of my wife,

Miriam Vassallo Nodar,

and her enduring presence.

You are always in my thoughts.

For anyone who's ever loved deeply, lost fully, and still found

the courage to begin again.

Table of Contents

CHAPTER 1

THE SEAM AT WARATAH SANDS

Daniel

Grief, it turns out, is excellent at directions. My counsellor told me to walk, so I did, not with purpose, just with surrender. I let the sadness point, and it dragged me like a tired dog down the cliff path to Waratah Sands Lighthouse.

I didn't plan to end up there.

The path simply curved that way, and I followed because turning back felt like a betrayal of whatever map sorrow had drawn for me. The air was full of salt, wind and memory. The kind of wind that leans in close, like an overfamiliar aunty determined to remind you how much weight you've lost. The ocean below was doing its old two-step: smoothing its stones, sharpening its knives.

I came because I wanted a view that could out-stare what was inside me.

The lighthouse obliged.

It stood there like a stubborn prayer.

Weathered bricks, paint salted and freckled, its iron railing thinned by the faith of too many hands. On a map, it's just a symbol.

In person, it's a throat clearing, a vertical defiance against the flat tyranny of sea and sky.

The winter light was beginning its evening rehearsal. The pewter sky softening to silver cloth, the horizon folding in on itself like a weary sigh. I sat on the bench, a paper cup of something too proud to be called tea warming my hands, and I tried to accomplish nothing.

Folks, that's harder than you'd think.

Doing nothing hurts if you've fallen out of practice.

It wants to hold its breath in slow motion.

Above me, the lens turned.

Slow as a thought you're afraid to let go of.

The glass caught the last of the sun and split it into syllables: there, there, there — whispered across the empty sea like an apology. A thin, precise line of cloud drew a false horizon across the true one, and for a moment I had the strange sense that the world had two skins, one pulled gently over the other.

Then the air shifted. Doubled, somehow.

Not colder. Not warmer. Just... different.

As though another room had been laid on top of this one, faint and translucent. The taste of metal brushed my tongue.

The hair on my arms voted unanimously for attention.

And that's when I saw her.

She stood on the far side of the boundary fence.

Straight-backed, coat the colour of damp sand, scarf knotted tightly as if the wind had been asking personal questions. She was looking up at the lantern with the expression people reserve for old machinery that's outlasted their contempt: exasperated respect.

When she turned, her eyes caught mine.

She looked at me the way someone might notice a bird caught at the edge of a photograph they thought they were taking of the sea.

"Who are you?" she asked.

"Daniel," I said, because names are what you throw across a gap when you have nothing else. "And you?"

"Eliza." Her vowels were familiar and not.

"Are you a keeper?"

"Not anymore," I said, glancing up at the solar gear and telemetry perched like prosthetics on the tower's crown.

 "No one is these days."

She followed my gaze, and her expression changed — expectation faltering into confusion. Her eyes swept the horizon as though the world should have had different furniture. Nothing but banksia and scrub and the lonely car park where tourists arrived to practice disappointment.

Her face went still with that polite blankness people wear when their brain says no but their eyes whisper here.

"Excuse me," she murmured, and stepped past me toward the path that, for me, ended in a sign about unstable cliffs.

For her, it seemed to lead home.

She didn't get far.

Five steps.

Then she froze, hands rising — half surrender, half praise.

Between us hung a seam.

I could almost see it.

Like the breath of a kettle, thin and deliberate.

The second horizon darkened, drew closer.

The air seemed to fold along an invisible crease.

I lifted my hand without meaning to. She did the same.

The seam hummed.

No, not a sound more like a shift.

It altered the key of the wind.

The universe's note changed.

"Do you see it?" I asked, afraid to blink.

"I do and I hear it." she said softly.

"What do you hear?"

"The wind," she said. "It's younger on my side."

Her smile was quick, shy, an apology for the strangeness, and a confession of belief.

"I can't explain it. It's simply true."

We stood there, two ghosts listening to an invisible hinge creak between worlds.

"What year is it for you?" I asked ridiculously and inevitably.

She thought for a moment, as if consulting some private barometer.

"Nineteen hundred and twelve."

I almost laughed, not from disbelief but from the sheer audacity of the universe.

"It's two thousand and twenty-six."

Eliza absorbed the number the way a coastline accepts a new tidemark.

The light above us turned again, slowly and solemnly.

The silver hour thinned. The second horizon trembled, then softened, and the seam unstitched itself until only the wind remained — single-layered, ordinary, indifferent.

She was gone.

I was alone again, with my bench, my paper cup, and the sea that repeats itself until you learn something.

You could say I imagined her.

People forgive that sort of thing in a grieving man.

But the air still tasted like a struck nail, and my palm remembered the polite refusal of that unseen barrier, and the wind had a new pitch, a subtle notch where before there had been none.

I went back the next night.

This time, I brought a fresh cup of tea and the foolishness of hope.

It is, after all, the only plan I've ever known that sometimes works.

If the world could open once, I told myself, it could open again.

I said that aloud, as though testing a rope, and the headland listened, patient as stone, without correcting me.

CHAPTER 2

THE LANGUAGE OF WEATHER

Eliza

Weather is a language, and the headland speaks it plainly. The low settled in June and made no promises. All that month we dried our coats in a row like penitent flags, the smell of salt and damp wool threading through the keeper's cottage.

The men, my husband, my brother-in-law, the others, measured patience by how they spoke to a stuck wick. I polished brass until my reflection grew shy. The woman who looked back at me had learned to take up less space and stand more firmly inside it.

I walked to the lighthouse when I needed to hear the world's skin creak. I walked to escape the roof that hoarded warmth and magnified every human sound, teacup clinks, restless sighs, words unspoken because they had been spoken too often before. I walked because, in some childish way, I believed that if I kept listening, the headland might one day say my name back.

It is vanity, yes, but it is also why we keep watches.

The first time I saw him, he sat like a question the wind had not yet decided how to answer. The seam shimmered between us. An invisible thread, impossible to pull, unbearable to break. When it closed, the air seemed to fold flat, neat, and the world felt new and thin. I went home and told no one. Wonders are happiest in the company of those who can see them.

The next evening, I returned, pretending even to myself that it was a coincidence. I brought a thermos and two enamel cups, because faith is made of ridiculous preparations.

The seam arrived like the tide, never exactly when you ask, and somehow at the precise right moment. The air thickened; the horizon doubled. Steam passed between us. Porcelain clinked against the absence. Our hands refused each other politely, like strangers on a narrow staircase.

He lifted his paper cup toward the seam; I lifted mine toward his. Tea met tea in a small, fragrant treaty.

"Tell me your year," he said.

"Nineteen hundred and twelve."

He closed his eyes, not to mourn the distance, but to honour how we were both alive inside it. "Two thousand twenty-six."

We stood within arithmetic and did not collapse.

I whispered the number to myself: two thousand twenty-six. A string of shells, a far-off rhythm. The lens above us took its breath and gave it back, turning slow as prayer. Below, the sea bit and smoothed, bit and smoothed, as it has always done.

"What keeps your light turning?" he asked.

"Duty," I said, then smiled.

"A weight on a clock. Oil and hands. The old things, still obliging."

"And you?" I asked.

"I am a keeper of fog," he said.

Half a joke, half a confession.

"I run a household and polish strangers' miracles and count how many steps it takes for the wind to get under the door."

He laughed softly then, and the seam approved, humming its quiet accord.

"Do you like it?" he asked.

"I like to be needed. I like the honest work of making glass remember how to shine. But some days I wish the world would widen." I answered.

The admission startled me; it startled him too.

The seam thrummed, tender and expectant, as though it knew that change begins with small betrayals of silence.

"What keeps you?" I asked to balance the ledger.

He told me about a mother who was dwindling but still laughed in the wrong places, which made the right ones survivable.

He said his work had once involved a desk and now involved a glowing screen, and some days the screen was kind, and some days it tried to eat the day whole.

He said grief had turned him into the sort of man who could sit on a bench, count a gull's wingbeats, and call it a use of time.

"You don't sound unhappy," I said.

"I don't," he agreed, bewildered by the truth of it. "I sound like the man who met you yesterday beside a line in the air and slept better because of it."

The seam thinned. There is never warning, just the feeling that the world has remembered an appointment.

We scrambled to make a plan in the narrowing space between breaths: this hour, again; this wind, if we can; any night the sea turns silver, and the light keeps time with its heart.

"If the wind changes key," I told him, "listen for me."

"I will," he said, and the way he said will sounded less like a promise and more like breathing.

Then the seam folded itself away.

The world clicked shut into one room again, leaving me with the thermos, the two foolish cups, and a pulse I could not still.

I laughed, low, disbelieving, because the impossible had learned our names and was now obliged to try again.

On my way back down the path, I picked a sprig of sea lavender. It stained my fingers violet. I pressed it later in my logbook between the pages that recorded the light's hours.

It felt like an offering to the future. A small, fragrant insistence that the world, once opened, might open again.

There is arrogance in that belief, and hope.

I have learned to wear both lightly, like a scarf a wind might steal.

CHAPTER 3

THE CONTRABAND OF LOVE

Daniel

On the third night I came bearing gifts, because love begins like smuggling: contraband tucked in a pocket, contrition at the ready.

Poetry—slim and immodest—fit inside my jacket, a collection of sonnets that had outlived their author but not their appetite. A pencil that smelled faintly of cedar insisted that the world was still made of trees. A sprig of wattle, gold as a small defiance, tried to out-yellow the day and failed—but cheerfully. I carried them to the bench, like a schoolboy with pockets full of pebbles he is dying to name.

The wind had turned mischievous, whistling through the scrub, tugging at my collar as if to say, You again? Above, the lighthouse blinked its single, patient eyelid, steady as an old priest who knows confession will come, eventually.

The seam arrived as if hired for the task—on cue, businesslike. The air doubled; the light thickened. There was that taste again, like struck iron and expectation. And there she was.

Eliza stepped into it with the sea behind her and a look that understood how fragile an hour could be. Even the wind seemed to hush around her. We lifted our cups again—silly, reverent, uncoordinated acolytes to something we didn't yet dare to name. Steam crossed. Our hands didn't.

"I brought you a book I can't pass," I said, the words feeling both absurd and necessary.

"Describe it," she said.

So, I did. I read three lines into the seam; the voice trembling at first, then evening out as if memory itself were listening. She closed her eyes and held the words like a mouth holds bread meant for someone else.

"Again," she said when I stopped, and I did—slowly this time, tasting each line before I gave it away.

Something in me nodded then, old and grateful, as though grief itself had set down its burden long enough to hear. We treated the poem like a small, nervous animal we hoped would stay.

When I finished, she smiled and reached into her coat pocket. "I brought something too."

She held up a button—mother-of-pearl, a little scuffed around the rim, gleaming like a moon with opinions about domestic labour. "From my coat," she said, "but it's too lovely to lose entirely."

Then she unfolded a piece of paper: a hand-drawn map of the headland, sketched with such care the paths looked like lines on a warm hand. "To make your future easier to live in," she said, and my laugh startled the seam into a richer note.

"You think my future is hard to live in," I said.

"I think everybody's is," she replied. "And that kindness makes it less."

I didn't know how to thank her except in the currency we'd invented. "There's a loose bolt halfway up the lighthouse stairs," I said. "Beneath it, a hollow of rust and spider dreaming. We could tuck notes there. Weather can't chew through iron."

Her eyes brightened with that delighted, cautious look people make when they recognise a conspiracy they can afford to join. "We could," she said. Then, softer: "We should."

We tested it. I wrote hello, you are extraordinary on a torn piece of receipt paper and fed it beneath the bolt with a twig from the banksia.

She went away by way of time and came back in terms of belief. When I checked the hollow, my note was gone. In its place lay a slice of ledger, edges crisp with age, ink like the tide's own handwriting:

You are kind. Keep being kind.

Something un-hunched in me. Not my spine— something deeper, more structural. I exhaled as if my lungs had been waiting for permission.

We spent the rest of that hour performing the practical magic of two people making a ritual out of fragments. We agreed on signs: the moon a thumbnail, the wind from the southeast, the swell speaking in its serious voice. She taught me to listen to the wind's key and hear when it changed its mind.

In return, I told her what the sea looked like from above when the light fell in ladders. She told me what it looked like from 1912, when lantern glass was still polished by hand, and the woman who tended it stood at the window holding the world steady with her looking.

"Who lit it tonight?" I asked.

"Mrs. Barker's boy," she said. "Under supervision with his mother's eyes." She paused, considering, then added, "I suppose all light is lit under supervision. Even the sun has its jealousies."

I loved her for sentences like that—for the way she lived inside words until they warmed to her. I loved her without deciding to, the way you love a familiar room that always smells faintly of the same good thing.

The seam wavered, its edges trembling like a curtain near the end of a performance.

"Do you keep a list?" I asked, trying to buy a little more time.

"Always," she said. "Don't you?"

"Always," I admitted, and pulled out my small notebook, foolish and proud. Lists are the quiet religion of the bereaved: if we can't keep the person, we keep the nouns around them.

She smiled, understanding without pity.

The next night, she showed me hers. Her handwriting was spare, precise, lovely: foghorn, baked custard, keeper's calendar, page 112 thumb-smudge, his voice when he says Darjeeling.

It was a life written in inventory. And yet, reading it, I saw the shape of the world she'd chosen to love.

That night I wrote my list with her in it: the seam's first hum; sea lavender stain; Eliza's careful map; the button that thought it was a moon; the old sentence becoming true—if the world opens once...

I forgot to drink my tea. The hour thinned. The second horizon softened its edges and faded.

"One more thing," she blurted, and in that instant, I saw the exact nature of us: she, precise even in wonder; me, greedy for one more moment.

"If the seam misbehaves," she said, "look for me when the moon is a thumbnail and the swell comes from the southeast. Listen for the wind. It changes key for us."

"It does," I said, as though I had always known.

We lifted our empty cups in a toast to absence. The seam breathed out and unstitched.

I sat for a long time after, list open on my knee, pencil caught in the crease like a finger marking a place I wasn't ready to lose. The bench creaked beneath me, and I fancied the wood had something to add and was choosing not to.

On the walk back, the path smelled of tea-tree and iron. Banksia cones rattled their dry laughter into the dark. The lighthouse clicked over to its serious night voice. In the car park, a lone tourist practiced his sighs at the stars.

At home, I put the book of poems on the table, the wattle in a glass, my hand on the fridge magnet that says

WARATAH SANDS in a typeface pretending to be rope. I thought of Eliza threading her way through lamplight to an iron stair where a note waited under a bolt, and I felt watched over by a kindness that exceeded the physics available to it.

If this is love, it has begun small and exacting and almost secret. It asks for listening and patience, for the humility of a bench and the willingness to be there when the wind changes key.

It asks me to bring tea I will forget to drink, to learn the headland's vocabulary, to hold a rope I cannot see and trust that someone is holding the other end.

Tomorrow, if the weather obliges, I will read her another poem. I will tell her the gull counted to eight before it changed its mind. I will press my thumb to her paper and pretend it is skin.

If the world can open once, it can open again.

I am learning to live as if that is not only a sentence, but a door.

CHAPTER 4

THE COLOUR OF HIS VOICE

Eliza

The sea was in a mood that evening, stamping its heels against the rocks and flinging foam as if to be noticed. The men called it a cross tide, but to me it felt more like impatience. An ocean trying to hurry the earth along.

All afternoon, the glass had been falling.

In the cottage, the keepers muttered about barometric omens, tightening ropes, checking shutters, filling the lamps. There was a metallic scent in the air the kind that comes before both lightning and truth.

I hurried up the slope with my thermos and my notebook; the wind chewing at my sleeves, tugging at my scarf until it came loose and snapped like punctuation. There is something curiously comforting in being bullied by the weather. It reminds you that you are alive and stubborn enough to stay that way.

When I reached the headland, he was already there.

Daniel.

With his coat turned up, his hair disobedient in the gale, he looked out toward the horizon as if it were a letter addressed to him. The light from the lantern brushed his face in moving stripes, bright, shadow, bright, like a heartbeat in motion.

When he turned and saw me, there was a flicker in his expression.

Relief so gentle it almost hurt to see.

No surprise.

No disbelief.

Just the quiet joy of something hoped for and finally delivered.

"I was afraid you wouldn't come," he said.

"I was afraid you would," I replied, smiling despite the wind's fingers in my hair. "Because then I'd have to believe it."

He laughed softly, the sound half-swallowed by the sea. And then, as if to honour the fragile courage between us, we poured tea.

Hands careful at the seam, we watched the steam cross again, mingling like breath.

The air hummed.

Thin, obedient, alive.

I felt the world make room for our small ceremony, as if it had been waiting all day for this very act of defiance: two people daring to meet between centuries, trading warmth across an invisible wound in time.

I showed him my notebook. "I started a list," I said.

"Of what?"

"Things to keep."

He smiled, and it was the sort of smile that had seen its share of losses. "May I hear some?"

I read aloud, voice trembling but steadying as the words gathered their rhythm:

"The foghorn's three-part moan. The scent of lamp oil. The keeper's calendar. The way Mrs Barker laughs when she swears she'll never bake again. The smudge on page one hundred and twelve of Persuasion. The colour of your voice when you say Darjeeling."

He blinked at the last one and looked down, flustered in the kindest way. "I never knew my voice had a colour."

"Everything has, if you watch long enough," I said. "Even shadows."

He chuckled, pulling a notebook from his coat, its edges damp from sea mist. "Mine's smaller," he admitted. "But it keeps me honest."

He flipped through pages filled with small, patient writing. "The gull that counts to eight before it gives up. The smell of rain on hot iron. Mum's laugh, even when it breaks. Eliza's map of the headland."

Hearing my name in his voice did something strange to the air between us. The seam thickened, the way air does just before a thunderclap.

It was as if my name had crossed time with more authority than the rest of me. I wanted to reach through that trembling barrier, to brush his sleeve, to see if he was as solid as the wind made him look.

The seam gave a warning hum, a sound like a struck tuning fork, and we both stepped back, laughing at our own restraint, embarrassed by how instinctively we'd leaned toward each other.

"If the world takes this hour from us," I asked, "what do we do?"

He looked toward the sea, thinking as the light strobed his profile in and out of being.

"We come back," he said. "Until it gives it back."

That was the moment I began to believe in him completely.

I closed my notebook.

"Then I'll keep that too," I said. "We come back."

The seam trembled once more, its hum growing softer, as though satisfied. The wind pressed its weight against my back, urging me toward the cottage, but I lingered.

When the air finally exhaled its slow, polite unthreading, I stayed where I was, tracing the empty space where he had stood. The lantern turned again above me, slow as prayer.

The sea's tantrum had gentled.

The foam folded back into rhythm.

The wind had changed its tune, lower now, more forgiving.

I wondered if that was the sound of hope when it learns your name.

I tucked my notebook under my arm and started back down the slope. The path glowed faintly with salt-light, and in every puddle, I saw a reflection of the lantern's long pulse, steady and alive.

At the foot of the tower, I checked the loose bolt where our secret lived. My heart stuttered at what I found: a new scrap of paper, damp but legible.

Your voice sounds like weather I'd wait out forever.

I pressed it to my chest, careful not to smudge the ink. Somewhere inside the lighthouse, Mrs Barker's boy was trimming the wick, and the flame flared, bright and certain.

I whispered, "Good night, Daniel," though I knew the seam had closed.

The words were not wasted.

The wind was listening.

When I reached the cottage, I laid his note beside my sea lavender and my mother-of-pearl button. Then I sat by the window, watching the light sweep across the dark, each rotation a slow, patient heartbeat.

If the world can open once, it can open again.

Tonight, it had opened wide enough for two voices, a list of small sacred things, and the colour of his voice saying Darjeeling.

CHAPTER 5

THE WEIGHT OF THE LIVING

Daniel

There are days when the living demands your attention.

Mum fell again, the nurse said over the phone. Nothing was broken, but they wanted me to come. So, I went—an hour's drive, wet roads, the radio doing its best to fill the silences between thoughts.

The clouds leaned low, heavy with something that hadn't yet decided whether to be rain or mercy.

At the care home she sat small in her chair, cardigan buttoned wrong, eating the soft part of a sandwich first. The way she always had.

"You came," she said, surprised.

"Of course," I said.

"Good. You can tell them to stop putting sugar in the soup."

We talked or tried to. Her mind drifted like a balloon that kept tugging at its string. Every so often, she'd glance up and say my name as if checking I was still attached to the world she remembered.

I stayed overnight, dozing in a chair while the television muttered weather reports to no one in particular. Grief is a quiet creature—it waits until you think you've kept it penned, then sits by your bed and breathes.

At dawn she was still asleep, mouth slightly open, the rise and fall of her chest the only proof that time hadn't taken her in the night. I kissed her forehead, straightened her cardigan buttons, and left before the carers began their morning rounds.

On the drive back, guilt rode shotgun.

The sky was late that evening, holding onto its light like a promise it wasn't ready to keep. I parked by the fence and hurried up the path, half afraid the seam would have lost interest in me. That whatever fragile geometry that held our worlds together might have given up on patience.

The bench. The lantern. The wind, restless as thought. And yes—the seam. But faint tonight, as though it had been waiting too long and grown shy. The air buzzed like a frayed wire.

She was there.

Eliza stood on the other side, coat whipping around her like it had something urgent to say. When she saw me, something eased in her face—an unguarded relief that reached me like warmth through glass.

"I thought perhaps it had gone," she said.

"Not yet."

The seam flickered; our voices caught between clarity and static. It reminded me of my mother's hearing aid before it gave up for good.

"I missed you," I said, louder than I meant to.

"I know," she said simply. "I felt it."

Her hand rose, palm out. I matched it. The invisible barrier hummed beneath our touch, and for an instant—just long enough to fool the heart—warmth passed through. Not contact, not really. But the suggestion of it, the ghost of closeness. The seam made a small sound, as if the world itself had gasped.

Then it let go.

The second horizon folded back into one, and she was gone.

I stood there longer than I should have, my palm still lifted to empty air. The sky had a bruised purple look, the sea heaving below as though impatient for me to leave.

That night I dreamed of holding a rope stretched across centuries. It hummed with the effort of being believed. I was pulling, always pulling, though I didn't know whether I was trying to bring her closer or keep myself from falling in. When I woke, my hand ached as if I'd been tugging all night.

I sat on the edge of the bed for a long time, listening to the house perform its small domestic miracles—the fridge humming, the pipes sighing, a bird arguing with its reflection in the window. Normal life, or the imitation of it.

I wondered what this thing with Eliza was turning me into.

Was it madness wearing a romantic disguise? Grief rearranging its furniture? Love? That seemed too bold a word for something so small, so tentative. And yet...

She had become the place where silence stopped hurting.

Still, I couldn't shake the unease. Every meeting was a kind of trespass. I was living two lives, one of pixels and grocery lists and visiting hours, and one of impossible physics and fragile devotion.

If she was real—and I believed she was, though belief had become a muscle that tired easily—what right did I have to reach across the years and ask her to keep doing this? To wait, to risk, to hope?

The next day, I went to the lighthouse in daylight for the first time in weeks. Tourists wandered the path; phones lifted like offerings. They walked past the bench without seeing the air quiver around it.

I stood by the fence, hands in pockets, feeling foolish. I thought about her coat, her lists, her voice saying Darjeeling. I thought about my mother, shrinking daily inside her chair, her sentences unravelling like dropped thread.

Two women separated by a century, both waiting on different kinds of mercy.

That night, I didn't bring tea or poems. I brought only myself, uncertain, weary, and a little afraid that the world might be ready to close its door.

When the seam finally appeared—late, reluctant—it was thinner than ever. I saw her only faintly, her outline flickering like a candle in its final millimetres of wax. She smiled, though, as if to steady me.

"Are you alright?" she asked.

"I don't know," I said. "The living are heavy."

"I know," she whispered. "We carry them too, sometimes."

Before I could answer, the seam shuddered and vanished.

The night cracked open with wind, and I gripped the fence post, breathing like someone who had run far and fast and found no finish line.

When I got home, I sat in the kitchen with the light off, the book of poems opened to the page I had meant to read her. The words blurred, but I didn't bother to wipe my eyes.

If the world can open once, it can close too.

I prayed—not in the old way, but in the way of a man who has no better vocabulary left—that it hadn't.

CHAPTER 6

THE WEATHER BETWEEN US

Eliza

Rain had pinned us indoors for three days straight. The men grumbled about the lamp wick, muttering that damp air made everything soft—metal, patience, tempers. Mrs Barker baked her frustration into scones, their edges crisp with fury. The cottage smelled of steam, sugar, and resignation.

I kept busy cleaning lenses that were already clean. It gave my hands something to do while my mind circled the same thought: Was he waiting?

The foghorn moaned every quarter hour like a reminder that the world was still larger than our small domestic noise. Each time it sounded, the sound pressed through the walls and through me, a low pulse from the sea itself: He's there. He's there.

On the third morning, the storm eased. The rain thinned to a mist that felt like breath. The clouds split reluctantly, and a small light appeared, raw and honest as forgiveness. I didn't even pretend to wait for the others to notice.

I climbed the path as if chased by sunlight.

The air still smelled of salt and soaked grass; the gulls were half hysterical with relief. My boots left prints in the soft earth, and the hem of my skirt gathered the scent of rain. By the time I reached the ridge, the wind had picked up its old habit of talking to itself.

The seam greeted me halfway, humming its expectant note—low, almost shy. It shimmered faintly, like glass misting over before a storm.

And there he was.

Daniel.

He stood with his hands in his pockets, pale with worry, his eyes shadowed from a night spent awake. The sight of him struck me like recognition—swift, unearned, absolute. I wanted to reach through time and smooth the crease from his brow, to tell him that concern looks better on other men, not on him.

"You look tired," I said.

"I am," he admitted. "But seeing you makes the hours make sense again."

The wind had softened; the sea was reciting itself more gently, as though tired of its own dramatics. We sat on either side of the seam, close as the rules of the world allowed.

There was a pause—the kind that isn't empty but waiting to become something.

"Tell me something true," he blurted.

I hesitated, my hand tightening around the thermos. "Once, I was to be married," I said. "His name was Henry. He had a kindness that frightened people because they didn't know where he kept it all. He died of fever before the banns were read."

"I'm sorry," Daniel said, and I believed him.

"I thought the world ended," I said. "But it only changed its handwriting. Now, when I polish the lamp glass, I think I'm smoothing the air between here and where he might be."

He looked at me carefully, as if memorising the shape of the space my sorrow occupied.

"And now?" he asked.

"Now I polish the air between here and you."

The words surprised me even as I said them. They came from a part of me that had long stopped asking for witnesses.

He smiled then, a soft, astonished thing, as if happiness were an animal that had come out of hiding. "You make the impossible sound reasonable."

"Isn't that what light does?" I asked. "It shows you what's there, even if it shouldn't be."

We fell quiet again, but it wasn't the silence of distance—it was the silence that comes when two people have already said enough.

His face was clearer tonight. The seam seemed thinner, as though the storm had rinsed away whatever dust clung to time itself. He looked older than the last time—his eyes carrying more night than day—but there was steadiness there too, the kind that holds when belief falters.

I wanted to tell him that every day of rain; I had written his name in the condensation on the cottage window, that I had whispered, wait for me to the foghorn, that I had dreamed in his century's language.

But I said none of that. Some truths are too tender to survive translation.

The seam faded. We both felt it before it moved, the air pulling back into itself like fabric cooling after an iron.

I leaned close, voice low. "I am glad I met you."

"I am glad you exist," he replied.

Then the air stitched itself closed.

I fell to my knees in the wet grass and laughed until my throat hurt, because joy, when you are not used to it, can feel a little like drowning.

The gulls wheeled above me, calling nonsense to the sky. Below, the sea was still muttering its thousand-year sermon about faith and forgetting.

When I rose, I wiped the mud from my palms and pressed one against the side of the lighthouse. The stones were warm; the light revolving inside steady as breath.

In that moment, I thought: He is the light I have been polishing toward all along.

And then, like every keeper who ever loved a dangerous thing, I remembered the rule we all learn too late—that every light which bridges the dark must eventually burn something.

CHAPTER 7

EXHIBIT A

Daniel

The lighthouse was no longer a lighthouse. It was an exhibit with plaques that began in 1912 and ended with the polite distance of modern fonts. You know the kind, earnest sans serif, a little too pleased with legibility, like a primary school teacher with laminated flashcards.

I hadn't planned to visit; grief makes you superstitious about pilgrimage.

But a friend texted—You've been cooped up.

Let's take a drive.

Coffee by the coast, and I heard myself say yes before I could consult the small, suspicious animal that lives behind my ribs.

So, there I was, standing in the foyer where school groups whispered around glass cases of polished brass and sepia photographs. A volunteer in a tidy fleece vest offered an audio guide with a disinfected smile.

The ticket printer stuttered out a barcode and a fact about focal lengths. The gift shop had tea towels printed with line drawings of the lantern and a tasteful rack of books with titles like Women of the Light: Unsung Lives at Sea's Edge.

I told myself I was only curious.

That it was only a building.

That buildings do not keep secrets for long.

But when I saw a sign with the words OIL ROOM pointing to the right stencilled above a narrow doorway, something inside me straightened, like a compass hearing its north.

I drifted along with the others.

Families corralling smaller weather systems of children, couples holding hands with the glandular confidence of the newly hopeful, two teachers doing headcounts with the terror of the nearly responsible. The floorboards creaked differently than I remembered from my night visits, lighter somehow, or perhaps more rehearsed. The air smelled of salt and varnish and the sensible sterility of museum cleaning fluid. Beneath that— something fainter. Dust, perhaps, or time's exhale.

The tour guide had a voice trained to travel: "If you look to your left, you'll see the historic domestic quarters restored to circa 1912. Notice the built-in settle by the hearth, typical of coastal worker cottages. Keepers' wives often polished the brass fittings to maintain the optic's performance and—according to some accounts—to find a sense of pride and purpose in a place that could be isolating."

Polished the brass.

The phrase caught, scratched, stayed.

I imagined Eliza's hands, salt-chapped, clever, working a cloth while the men swore at a stubborn wick. I let the group eddy past and pretended to read a sign about paraffin standards and wicks-per-week. On the wall, a photograph: a woman half turned from the camera, face unreadable, light falling in a soft band across her shoulder. The caption called her "Unidentified Keeper's Wife, 1912." I had the unfaithful thought that perhaps captions sometimes lie out of mercy.

We stepped into the oil room: low ceiling, shelves like sober scripture, a reconstructed rack holding dented cans with labels that now looked theatrical—BEST QUALITY OIL— and a placard explaining the difference between colza and paraffin. Oil dripped slow from a spout into a demonstration measure.

A child asked, "Does it smell?" and the guide said, "When it burns, yes," and I thought: It smells like duty and warmth and the price of sight.

My friend wandered off in search of coffee, or escape, or both. I followed the tour as far as the keeper's cottage and then let their bodies screen me while I drifted behind to the fireplace. Here, the museum had restored cosiness starting with a rag rug, a table set with enamel cups, and finally a mended chair whose mend was prettier than the original wood. Authenticity curated to be both accurate and acceptable, like a scar in good light.

That's when I saw it.

A small alcove by the fireplace, where the plaster had flaked away to expose an older layer beneath.

A museum label nearby noted: Original masonry visible following 2024 stabilization works. The words skimmed past me. The sight didn't.

Behind the loosened brick—paper.

Fragile, browning, folded small.

My heart stuttered. I knew that fold.

The neatness, the deliberate corners. Eliza's kind of fold. The seam had taught me how you can recognise a person not only by their voice or gait but by the way they close a thing for safekeeping.

I checked over my shoulder and saw no one watching except the benevolent eyes of history.

I eased it free, breath hitching as if air itself might be loud enough to betray us. The paper sighed in my hands, a dry whisper of long-kept things. The ink had bled with the years; the lines feathered as though the words had grown fur to keep from freezing. But the message was unmistakable:

If you are reading this, you are a stranger or someone like us—a person bent by weather. Please be kind to this place. It looks after us.

I couldn't breathe for a moment.

A schoolchild brushed past me, laughing, and the sound felt obscene, like a ringtone during a requiem. I refolded the note along its old obedient seams and slid it back, the way you return a bird to a nest you have no right to know.

I pressed my fingers against the rough brick as if it might pulse with life.

I wanted fiercely to take it.

To hold proof.

To have a thing that said, You are not unwell; the world is. But I knew what Eliza would say, could hear her voice with that amused firmness that made me love her more: Do not steal from time, Daniel. It has already given enough.

So, I left it where it belonged, between the wall's two centuries, tucked into the house like a promise.

The associate professor ushered the group onward.

"In this room, children would have done chores such as—" The rest merged into a neutral narrative-current. Outside, the sea flashed silver through museum glass.

A sign on the wall said KEEPERS' LOG — 1912–1918 in a font that cared about clarity and not at all about longing.

Inside the display case, a hand with careful ink had recorded weather and bearings and practical continuities. I thought of her name, unwritten there but alive between the lines. I stood in the middle of the restored room, surrounded by the ghosts of function, and understood with a slight shock I was the exhibit. A man peering at his own hunger through a scrim of interpretation.

In the gift shop, I bought nothing and felt virtuous about it, the way you do when the thing you want is not for sale. My friend reappeared with a takeaway coffee and news about a new bakery in town that did scandalous things with cardamom. I nodded, said something about cardamom being the flirt of spices, and drove us back along the coast road while the sea played at being endless.

He asked gently, as good friends do, if I was sleeping. I said sometimes.

He asked if I was still going up there at night. I said sometimes.

He asked if I had talked to a counsellor lately. I said the word booked and let it idle between us like a car in neutral.

We passed a billboard for a retirement village with a smiling couple who looked well paid for their serenity. I thought about Mum's cardigan buttons, the way grief made her mouth forget how to finish words. I wondered which world I was failing by loving the other.

At home, the kitchen was the same as ever: the tired magnet that says WARATAH SANDS in rope-pretend font, the poem book open where I'd left it, and on the table a grocery list written in my careful grief-hand: milk, bread, bin liners, soap, biscuits.

The normalcy felt like a trick pulled by an impish god. I made tea I did not drink and stood by the window until the light thinned to its pewter rehearsal.

Doubt, which had been hovering for days like weather offshore, came in.

What exactly were we doing?

What shape could this be stretched across a century?

There were no words for it that didn't feel either adolescent or metaphysical. I thought about boundaries, not only of time but of good sense. I thought about Eliza's life, its stitched obligations, its careful dignity.

Was I asking her to risk something she would have to pay for?

Was she asking the same of me? Every miracle has a ledger; someone, somewhere, keeps the accounts.

Evening gathered with a shy insistence lighthouses understand.

I drove back because not going would have been another kind of superstition, and anyway the car seemed to know the way by heart. The car park had two vehicles sulking into the dark. The wind tasted of wet stone and a promise of colder nights. I climbed the path, the bench, the fence—the catechism of approach.

The seam arrived thin and punctual, like a line on a ledger that doesn't yet know what number it must hold. The world doubled in the familiar hush.

Eliza was there, a little blurred, like a photograph printed on soft paper. Her coat, her steady posture, the concentration that is her kindness.

"I wasn't sure it would find us," she said.

"Today, it found me somewhere else," I said. "Inside the cottage. Behind a brick."

Her breath caught. "Oh."

"I didn't take it," I blurted, in case she had the thought and needed relief from it. "I put it back."

Her face, my God, the relief there, was almost more than I could stand.

"Thank you," she said. "Some things are safer in the wall."

We sat, or the seam's version of sitting, as near as rules allowed. The wind had moderated into a grown-up conversation with the grass. Below, the sea recited its catechism in a smaller voice.

"Tell me," she said, "what it said."

I recited it to her, the way one does a prayer one hopes not to misquote.

When I finished, she smiled as if someone had finally remembered her birthday. "That sounds like me," she said. "I am a great advocate for places."

"You are a place," I said before I could edit the thought. "Or rather, you make one."

She considered that with the seriousness of a person deciding where to put a nail in a supporting wall.

"I hope I am not a place that costs more than it gives."

"Some places pay for themselves in light," I said, and felt foolish and true at once.

We talked about small things then, because big ones bring the seam too near its limits: Mrs Barker's scones ("They are better when she is angry," Eliza confided); my friend's cardamom bakery (I tried to explain cardamom; she said, "Like a scandalised angel?" and I said exactly); the tour guide's script; the way children leave fingerprints that look like proof of presence on glass, which is perhaps all any of us leave.

There were moments, lit and shadowed both, when doubt pressed its thumb into my certainty. I heard myself ask, "What do we do if this remains, well, only this?"

The sentence wobbled like a ladder on uneven stone.

She stared at me.

"We let it only do more work than it knows how," she said. "We let this be the size it insists on being. If it grows, we grow with it. If it doesn't, we don't scold it for being small."

I wanted to tell her about Mum's fall, about the soup too sweet, about feeling like a man living two contradictory truths and paying a full price for both.

I wanted to confess the museum feeling, the sudden knowledge that I was the one under glass. But the seam shivered; the hour thinned.

"Before it goes," I said quickly, "I want to try something practical."

The word practical was our talisman. Magic we could name without frightening it.

She tilted her head. "Go on."

"I'll write to you on the stair," I said. "Under the loose bolt. Not a poem—just words to hold fast. If the seam misses its appointment, you'll have something." I swallowed. "I'll have something too."

She nodded, solemn as a treaty. "Tonight?"

"Tonight," I said.

The seam inhaled, a delicate tremor before the world remembered it preferred to be one thing. "Daniel," she said.

"Yes?"

"Thank you for not taking the note." Her voice lifted, almost shy. "It would have broken my heart in a very modern way."

We smiled, which felt like a luxury you can't buy even in a wonderful gift shop. Then the air unstitched, polite as always, and the headland resumed its single mind.

I went up.

Inside, the museum had gone quiet in the way curated spaces do after hours as when exhibits settle back into their private faces, labels unconcerned with comprehension. A security light draped the stair in respectable gloom. Halfway up, my hand found the loose bolt as reliably as a prayer finds its line. The hollow beneath felt the same—ancient flakes of paint, the tickle of a spider's abandoned attempt, a small coolness like kept breath.

From my pocket, I took the paper I'd folded and refolded until it held the shape of decision. I wrote only three words, neat as I could, the cedar pencil making its soft, human scratch.

I found you.

I fed the slip into the hollow with the care you give fragile birds and necessary lies. The bolt settled above it with its familiar grudging squeak. For a long moment I kept my fingers there, as though warmth were a courier with a duty to perform.

On the way down, the exhibit felt less sure of itself.

The plaques seemed to read me for once.

In 2026, a man came often and tried to learn how to live. The foyer still smelt of varnish and commerce; the gift shop had shut its eyes and counted its till; the tea towels hung like compliant flags. Outside, the sea resumed its silver practice, and the wind rehearsed tomorrow.

In the car, my phone lit with a message from the care home: Your mother had a settled evening. Sleeping now.

I closed my eyes and thanked every minor god of corridors and night staff and soup unsweetened.

When I opened them, the lighthouse had already become itself again and the museum's edges invisible in the dark; the beam writing its old essay across the water.

On the drive home, the radio offered a song I didn't recognise about the odds of love. I turned it down and let the car hold me between two kinds of quiet.

At a red light, I touched my palm to my sternum, an old habit from a life that needed body checks, and felt the low, reasonable thud of a heart that, against probability, still considered its work worthwhile.

Back at the kitchen table, I left the poem book closed. I wrote bin liners on tomorrow's list again and, beneath it, an item no grocer could supply patience.

Then I stood by the window until the house confessed its small noises, and the horizon lost the last of its detail.

Just before sleep, I tried to imagine her finding the note: the soft, efficient press of her fingers; the way her mouth would crease when she read the words aloud to herself; the care with which she would fold the paper back along its corners so it would learn how to be kept.

I pictured her saying, 'He found me', and for once the sentence didn't feel like presumption.

It felt like a fact with its shoes off.

If the world can open once, it can open again.

Museums and walls and bolts and years are only different costumes for the same old door. Tonight, I did not pray. I made a — let's call it a deposit.

Small, exact, into the ledger that kindness keeps.

And then, for the first time in a week, I slept.

CHAPTER 8

THE MOMENT ENTIRE

Eliza

He had written; I found you. And below, a small drawing of a heart though not the kind that appears on Valentine cards or stitched into samplers. His heart was all geometry and intent, shaped like a lighthouse lens: concentric circles, delicate lines that implied both structure and mercy. I laughed aloud, startling the gulls from the parapet. They rose in a sudden chorus of wings, indignant at joy.

I held the note against the lamplight, its edges trembling in the sea wind. The pencil marks had softened with damp, but the meaning was still fierce. I imagined him kneeling at the stair, hands careful, pressing paper into the hollow beneath the bolt, as though building an altar out of iron and time. I could almost smell the cedar of his pencil.

That evening, the seam came bright and eager; the air tinged with copper as if struck by an unseen bell.

The sea was calm but expectant, like a congregation holding its breath before the hymn.

He was already there.

Daniel stood closer than ever before, his coat caught in the wind, eyes wide with something between awe and terror. The surrounding air shimmered with the density of unsaid things.

"I think it's trying," he said.

"Trying?"

"To let us through."

The hum deepened.

Resonant as a cello string drawn slow by a careful hand. Even the gulls stilled. The wind quieted to the attentive hush of a room waiting for prayer. The horizon rippled, unsteady as glass under heat.

Then, astonishingly, the air softened.

For a heartbeat, just one, we were in the same room.

I reached forward before reason could protest, and my hand met his.

Actual skin, real skin, warm and human, not imagined. The shock of it made us both gasp, as though the air itself had bitten us in its wonder.

I could feel the tremor in his fingers, the thrum of a pulse that said: Yes, I am here. Yes, I am alive.

The world had cracked open and decided not to explain itself.

We stood like that, too startled to speak, two people holding a fact the universe had forgotten to forbid. The seam quivered around us, unsure whether to celebrate or recoil. I looked into his face and saw disbelief fighting joy—and losing.

Then, as swiftly as it had come, the air tightened.

The seam snapped back, flinging us apart into our respective hours with the indifference of a closing door.

I stumbled against the railing, breathless and laughing. He mirrored me on his side, pressing both hands to his face, his shoulders shaking in something between laughter and shock.

Below, the sea roared approval like a wild, uncontainable applause.

When I could finally speak, I whispered, "It worked."

He nodded, still shaking. "It worked."

For a long time, we said nothing else.

The silence felt fragile, newly minted. Every sound seemed too loud for it—the sigh of the tide, the creak of the lantern, even the small rasp of breath.

At last, we spoke again, our voices soft and conspiratorial, like children who had broken a rule and found it worth the trouble.

We talked about the conditions: the phase of the moon, the angle of the wind, the smell in the air just before the hum changed key. We noted it all like scientists mapping a miracle, convinced that method might coax it back.

"We should try again," he said. "Record everything. Build a pattern."

I smiled, though my hand still trembled. "A Map of Miracles."

He chuckled, the sound full of wonder and fear in equal measure.

But even as I spoke, as we charted and planned, something inside me knew the truth.

The world does not repeat its tenderness.

Time is generous, not kind.

It offers once, and once only.

The seam began to fade.

We both felt it retreat.

The pressure easing, the shimmer loosening its hold on the air. The wind returned, disoriented by its absence.

I touched my palm and felt the warmth lingering there—the impossible made tactile.

The skin remembered more than the mind could bear.

He was already vanishing, his outline softening, his eyes full of the question neither of us dared to ask: What now?

When the light thinned to ordinary, I pressed that same hand to my heart and made myself a promise: If I could not keep him, I would keep the moment entire.

Later, in the keeper's logbook, I wrote without explanation: Weather: wind southerly, tide moderate. Visibility: beyond measure. Event: contact made.

Mrs Barker would read it in the morning and think me fanciful, but it didn't matter.

Some truths are not meant to be understood.

That night, I could not sleep.

The lamp turned in its slow revolutions above me, washing the ceiling in restless gold. I held my hand to the light, watching it as it passes through the spaces between my fingers, and thought: So, this is what it means to be seen.

I thought, too, of Henry.

His kind eyes, the quiet way he had once folded my name into a letter that never reached me because fever took him first. And I realised with a strange calm that love does not cancel itself out over time; it accrues, like light inside a lens. It gathers until the heart can no longer distinguish what belongs to then and what belongs to now.

I wondered what Daniel was doing in his century.

If his heart still raced the way mine did, if he was looking at his hand and thinking how absurd and holy touch can be.

I whispered into the dark, "You found me," though the air had no seam to answer.

Outside, the sea was practicing calm again, its anger spent. The gulls slept, their heads tucked beneath wings that knew better than to question the morning.

In the stillness, I remembered his drawing, the heart like a lens, the proof that even love can learn to refract.

I pressed my palm flat on the page of my notebook and traced the outline of my hand. Beneath it, I wrote: He is real. I am real. The world forgot to say no.

Then I closed the book, blew out the lamp, and let the dark settle. Gentle, complete, and still trembling with the echo of his touch.

Tomorrow, I will polish the lens again.

Not because it needed it, but because every turn of the cloth would remind me that somewhere, in another hour, another world, another heartbeat he was standing at the edge of the same light.

CHAPTER 9

THE VOW OF WEATHER

Daniel

Love can make even silence feel inhabited. For weeks the seam behaved, coming and going with an almost bashful precision.

We never summoned it.

It arrived when it wished, departing like a polite guest who refused to overstay. Our meetings were small miracles dressed in routine: a flicker of light, a breath held, and then the hum—low, sure, familiar.

We had learned the rhythm of it.

The seam wasn't ours to command, but we treated it gently, as one does an animal that startles easily.

We didn't ask questions of it anymore; we simply met whenever it pleased, like two travellers sharing the same inn at opposite ends of the century.

During those weeks, I caught myself living differently. The world looked less stable but more alive. Even my mother's care home seemed warmer, her fragile laughter less a sorrow and more a rhythm I could live beside. I wrote to Eliza under the loose bolt each evening, small words folded like prayers: still here, the moon's a thumbnail, your sea smells like memory. She always answered, her notes a mixture of wit and reverence, ink neat as devotion.

"I am happy," I mumbled to myself.

One evening, the air felt tender, washed clean by rain. The kind of evening that makes the world seem undecided— half daylight, half dream. I walked up the path with my usual mixture of superstition and hope.

The lighthouse loomed, its beam carving deliberate language across the dark, and the sea was murmuring its usual argument with the rocks.

She was already there.

Eliza stood with her hair caught in the wind, her hands wrapped around her thermos as if it contained the century itself.

That look again.

The one she wore when she'd already decided to be brave. The bravery that isn't loud, but patient, knowing it may have to break something gentle to stay true.

I stopped just short of the seam.

Words came before permission.

"Marry me," I said.

Her head tilted, uncertain whether to laugh. "You forget yourself, Daniel. I am a woman in another year."

"I don't forget," I said. "I remember too much. It doesn't have to be legal or sensible. Just true."

She stared at me through the trembling air.

The light refracted between us, bending her outline the way heat bends distance. "You mean like a vow."

"Yes," I said. "To call this what it is. To stop pretending it's smaller than it feels."

Her smile began slowly, like dawn rehearsing itself. "You and your reckless modern notions."

I took a step closer.

"You once said light shows you what's there, even if it shouldn't be. That's what this is."

She considered that, and then the smile deepened.

"Very well. A vow, then."

The air thickened in approval.

The seam pulsed once, its hum rising an octave, the wind turning reverent.

We stood facing each other, our hands hovering where the seam trembled, close enough that I could feel the warmth of her through the distortion, the press of presence that lived between touch and faith.

"I vow," I said, my voice low, "to remember your voice when the wind changes key."

Her eyes shone in the reflected light. "I vow," she said, "to keep polishing the air between us, so it never clouds."

"I vow," I said, "to call this love, even when time forgets the word."

"And I," she said softly, "to live as if we are possible."

The seam shivered, its tone deepening like a breath drawn after prayer.

For a long moment we simply looked at each other, two halves of a single courage, daring to believe that the world could stretch far enough to hold us both.

Then, with the gentle finality of closing a book, she whispered, "witness and weather have wed us."

And I replied, "So let the light keep watch."

Something passed through the seam then, something invisible but undeniable.

The air brightened, not in glare but in conviction. The lighthouse beam swept over us both at once, a long benediction of gold and salt.

For that instant, the distance between centuries was no more significant than the space between one breath and the next.

We stood in silence, listening to the world adjust around what it had just permitted. Then the hum softened, loosening its grip on the air, and the seam began its familiar retreat. Neither of us moved to stop it. Some things must close to prove they ever opened.

When I turned back down the path, the rain had started again, a delicate percussion that matched the beat in my chest. The air smelled of wet iron and eternity. The sea, instead of taunting, kept time for us, each wave a vow repeated, untranslatable but certain.

In my pocket, beneath the warmth of my hand, her last note waited under the bolt: Tomorrow, if the wind changes key, listen. It may be us breathing.

I must have read it a dozen times before the path gave way to the car park, before the sound of tyres on wet gravel replaced the hush of the sea.

That night, I lay in bed and listened to the rain on the roof, steady and alive. It was the same rhythm I imagined she heard on her side, the 1912 version of the same storm, the same percussion on different tin.

I thought of her vow: to live as if we are possible.

And I realised that was the truest prayer I had ever heard.

Sleep took me slowly, like the tide reclaiming a stubborn shore. And just before I drifted off, I felt it—that small, impossible thing.

The air changed key.

And I knew she was listening.

CHAPTER 10

THE TIN OF FOREVER

Eliza

The lighthouse had a way of holding secrets. Behind every panel and under every stair there were small pockets of history—an old pipe, a nail, the ghost of a keeper's shoe print. You could live a lifetime here and still not find all the places where the past tucked itself away for safekeeping.

I left ours there too.

That morning the sea was behaving itself—only mildly irritable, like a child forced to sit through church. The air smelled of lamp oil and fresh bread, a combination that always makes me feel slightly virtuous, as though domesticity were a moral achievement.

I spent the morning cleaning the lamp, polishing the brass until the glass burned back my reflection. There's a kind of vanity in that task—pretending the light depends on you when, in truth, it has always known how to shine. When the lamp was trimmed and ready for evening, I took a small tin from the kitchen cupboard.

It had once held barley sweets—the kind that stick to your teeth and remind you to be patient with pleasure. The label was long gone, but if you tilted it just right, you could still smell sugar and a hint of nostalgia.

Inside, I placed a folded sheet of paper—the list of "Things to Keep" that Daniel and I had built line by line across the seam. I read it aloud one last time, as if rehearsing a prayer:

The sound of the seam's first hum
Sea lavender stains
His laugh when he says my name
The colour of a storm at dusk
The promise that time can bend for love

I sealed it with wax from the lamp because I liked the symmetry of it—the light keeping our words safe. The wax dripped unevenly, forming a lump that looked, I thought, rather like an ear. Not romantic, perhaps, but practical; love should listen as well as glow.

When no one was watching, I slipped into the oil room. The air there always smelled of ghosts and paraffin—an excellent combination if you enjoy feeling haunted and industrious at once. I moved the crooked shelf (which squealed like a tattletale) and tucked the tin behind it.

"Stay hidden," I whispered, as if it were a living thing.

Mrs Barker nearly caught me on the way out. She was carrying a tray of tea and suspicion. "You're up to something," she said.

"I'm preserving history," I replied.

She squinted. "History rarely requires that much wax."

I smiled sweetly. "Neither does good company."

That disarmed her long enough for me to retreat before I had to invent a reason why my hands smelled of barley and eternity.

The next evening, the wind settled into that silvery tone we'd come to recognise—the one that meant the world was feeling hospitable. The seam appeared, humming its expectant note, and Daniel stood waiting. He always looked a little undone at first, as though the air between centuries mussed his sense of balance. His hair never quite obeyed the laws of either time or gravity.

"I left you something," I told him, smiling.

"A problem?" he asked, hopeful.

"A piece of us," I said. "For when you find it."

He frowned, puzzled. "When?"

"Whenever time decides you need reminding that we were real."

He tilted his head, and the light caught his face in a soft, impossible way it sometimes does. The look of someone halfway between laughter and prayer.

The seam trembled, uncertain. "You sound as if you think this won't last," he said.

"Nothing lasts," I replied. "That's what makes it precious."

He looked at me through the shimmer, and the sadness in his eyes was almost holy. Then, because sadness can't bear to be taken too seriously, I added, "Besides, if this all collapses, at least you'll have a fine excuse for missing anniversaries."

That made him laugh—an honest, startled sound that seemed to pull light straight through the air between us. I could feel it in my bones.

"Then we'll last through remembering," he said, once the laughter settled.

"Through remembering," I echoed. "And possibly through excellent filing systems."

The seam pulsed gently, as if approving of our foolishness. For a few minutes we spoke of ordinary things— the state of the sea, the curious ambitions of seagulls, how he'd once attempted to bake bread and produced instead a geological specimen. The world loves to hide the profound inside the ridiculous.

When he was gone, I stood for a long time watching the lantern turn. The beam swept across the sea, steady as a heartbeat, reaching for ships that might never come.

I realised then that love is not the light itself.

It's the turning.

The persistence of it.

The willingness to keep sweeping the dark, again and again, in case someone out there needs to be found.

I touched my palm, where his had once been, and felt the faintest warmth still there, stubborn as hope.

"Keep watch," I whispered to the lamp. "He will find us."

And somewhere far ahead—or perhaps far behind—the wind changed key, as if to say, I already am.

CHAPTER 11

QUIETER ROOMS

Daniel

Mum died in the spring. The nurse said she went quietly, as though that were consolation. I suppose that's what we say when the world ends politely. I sat by her bed for a long time after they'd gone, holding her hand long after it cooled, telling her all the things I'd forgotten to when she could still hear me.

That she'd done her best.

That she'd taught me kindness, even when I didn't deserve it.

That I'd met someone—strange as it sounded—who made me feel alive again.

Her fingers were thin and birdlike, and when I let go, they seemed to take flight into some gentler air.

The funeral was small and polite.

Tea in white cups, ham sandwiches, conversations that tiptoed around emotion. People said she'd had a good innings, as if life were a game that duration could win. The vicar spoke of peace; I thought of stubbornness. She had both, though never in equal measure.

Afterward, I drove to the lighthouse because I had nowhere else to take the ache.

The wind was sharp that day, the kind that felt freshly laundered. The sky had been rinsed clean, and the horizon looked almost too far away for comfort. I parked where I always did, beside the sign that said Waratah Sands Heritage Site, and walked up the familiar path with the certainty of ritual.

When the seam opened, it came softly—no flash, no grandeur, just a shift in the wind's key, a change in the air's colour. And there she was.

Eliza.

Coat buttoned high, cheeks pink from the cold, her face lit by the pale gold of the lantern. Seeing her was like stepping into the part of a dream that still makes sense.

"I felt something change," she said softly. "Was it your mother?"

I nodded. Words failed me, and she didn't fill the silence. She never does. She only looked at me with that steady compassion that makes you brave enough to breathe again.

For a long moment, the wind said everything I couldn't.

"Tell me about her," Eliza said finally.

So, I did.

I told her about the woman who whistled in the kitchen while burning toast, who called lorikeets little drunks, who kept all the twist-ties from bread bags in a jar because "you never know when the world will need more order." I told her how Mum laughed through bad news and sighed through good, as though she couldn't quite trust happiness not to spill.

"She sounds remarkable," Eliza said.

"She was ordinary," I replied.

"Then remarkable twice over."

Her voice was so calm that it made the words feel factual, like something you might read from a well-worn ledger.

I told her how Mum used to garden without gloves, saying the soil preferred to know who was handling it. How she'd fallen in love twice and forgiven once. How she'd taught me that grief doesn't end—it just finds quieter rooms.

Eliza listened as if each word were a pearl she intended to keep polished. When I finished, she reached toward the seam, her hand hovering an inch from mine. "Then we will remember her together," she said.

Something loosened in my chest. The ache shifted, still heavy but less alone.

I wanted to thank her, but instead I asked about the tin.

"You said you left something behind," I said.

Her smile was secretive, the kind that suggested amusement and conspiracy in equal measure. "You'll know when you find it."

"I already have," I said.

And for once, she didn't argue.

The seam flickered then, as if shy of its own tenderness. The air between us pulsed faintly, neither open nor closed, just thinking about it. We didn't speak again, but she reached forward and brushed the air where our hands would have met.

The wind responded—a low, affectionate murmur, the sound of two centuries shaking hands.

When the seam finally faded, I stayed there longer than usual, the bench damp under me, the world both sharper and softer than it had been an hour before.

The sea was loud that night, the kind of loud that isn't threatening, just emphatic—like an old friend interrupting your thoughts to remind you it's still there. A gull circled once, cried out, and then seemed to reconsider whatever it was about to say.

I laughed. Out loud. Alone. And it didn't sound strange.

On the walk back to the car, I caught myself talking to Mum the way I used to when she was half-listening from another room. "You'd have liked her," I said. "Or at least, you'd have wanted to feed her."

By the time I reached home, the first real chill of evening had set in. The kettle took its time; the house felt too large, and everything smelled faintly of soap and memory.

I took the small notebook where I kept our notes—the one smudged with salt and thumbed with use—and wrote:

She knew. Before I said a word, she knew.

And for the first time since the hospital, I slept without dreaming of goodbye.

When I woke the next morning, light filled the room in a way that made it appear the world had been scrubbed overnight. The wind outside had changed key again.

I listened.

And there it was—so faint I almost missed it—the low, familiar hum that meant the world was still listening back.

CHAPTER 12

THE TILT OF THE WORLD

Eliza

The world tilts quietly before it changes. You rarely notice until you look up and everything has shifted a few centimetres to the left.

In August 1914, the news came.

War in Europe.

The word rippled through the coastal towns like a contagion.

The men talked of duty; their voices threaded with something between pride and fear.

The women packed trunks, wrapped breakables in old newsprint, and spoke briskly so their hands wouldn't tremble. Even the sea seemed uncertain in its colour, duller, its confidence thinned.

The headland, usually so sure of itself, felt suddenly smaller.

We were to be reassigned inland for a time, to help with supply postings and coded communications.

"Temporary," they said, but in wartime, every temporary is a question without a mark at the end.

I wanted to refuse, to argue that light was its own form of service. Those ships still needed to find their way home, even in a world gone mad.

But there was no refusing the tide of history.

The order bore a signature that did not care about sentiment.

The night before we left, I went to the lighthouse one last time.

The air was taut and expectant.

Clouds were gathering with the confidence of bad news. I climbed the spiral staircase, every step echoing with the ache of leaving. The lens had already been half-shrouded for refitting, its great glass eye blindfolded like justice.

When the seam appeared, it was faint and flickering, like a candle nearly out of wick.

Daniel's face wavered on the other side, blurred by distance or grief or both.

"They're moving us," I said. "The light's being refitted."

His expression faltered. "How long?"

"I don't know," I said. "Weeks. Months, maybe more."

He ran a hand through his hair, and for the first time, he looked as untethered as I felt. "Eliza, don't let this be the last."

"It won't be." I wanted to sound certain, but the words came out brittle.

And even as I said them, the seam faded, shrinking like a breath being drawn back into the chest of time.

"Listen to me," I blurted. "If I can't come, I'll leave a note under the bolt. And if the wind carries it away, please know that I meant to. Know that I tried."

"Promise me," he said.

"I promise."

Then the seam gave a final pulse of light, a heartbeat, and a farewell in one, and folded shut.

I stood for a long time staring at my reflection in the dark glass of the lantern.

One woman caught between two wars, one of nations, one of years.

The silence that followed was almost cruel.

The next evening, the storm broke.

The headland howled.

Rain came in sheets so fierce it blurred the sea into sky. I pressed my last note beneath the bolt before the water could smear the ink. My handwriting was rushed but legible, the words an anchor against the inevitable:

Forgive me. Tomorrow I will be more yours.

The wax seal refused to set in the damp, so I muttered at it the way Mrs Barker mutters at her dough—persuasion through insult.

"Oh, come on then, you stubborn lump of virtue."

When that didn't work, I held the tin lantern close and hissed.

"You're worse than a child on Sunday."

The wax relented with a sigh and hardened, and I allowed myself to laugh once, because defiance is a good last sound.

But the next night, the seam did not appear.

Nor the night after.

The air, where it used to hum, was only air.

The silence of an empty instrument.

Mrs Barker said I was restless, though she used the word as if it were a sin. She tried to distract me with scones, which is the traditional prescription for heartbreak, but even buttered comfort cannot mend the sound of absence.

So I went back to the fence, night after night.

I pressed my hands against the wire until my palms burned.

"You are somewhere in time with me," I whispered, because to say it aloud was to keep it breathing.

The wind took it, carried it out to sea, and brought it back again.

Over and over, like a vow rehearsed by the waves.

And though I knew better, I answered.

"Yes," I said to the horizon. "Yes, I am here."

One night, I thought I heard his voice, a thin thread, caught between gusts. It could have been the wind, or grief playing mimic. Either way, it was enough to make me smile.

War changes everything, but it never quite knows what to do with love. Love is too domestic, too impractical to enlist. Yet there I was, marching orders in my hand, heart still stationed at the edge of the sea.

I packed quietly.

My notebook went into the trunk with my uniforms. The tin of barley sweets stayed behind in the oil room, hidden behind the crooked shelf. Inside it, our list—the record of what the world could be when it forgot to be impossible.

Before dawn, as the cart waited below, I climbed the lighthouse stairs one last time. The glass caught the faintest hint of morning, like a coin of light being flipped between worlds.

"I will come back. Even if I have to argue with time itself." I told the empty air.

The wind answered, as it always did, practical and unsentimental: Then be quick about it.

I laughed, wiped the mist from my face, and whispered, "Tell him I'm trying."

When I stepped outside, the sea was already brighter, pretending innocence after the night's rage. Somewhere, I hoped, Daniel felt the same wind, that same tilt of the world— a shared breath stretched impossibly thin across history.

And though the headland was shrinking behind me, the light still turned. Slow, patient, unwavering. A habit older than grief.

I promised myself then that as long as the beam still reached the water, he would never be entirely lost.

CHAPTER 13

THE HEAT BETWEEN WORLDS

Daniel

Summer came loud. It came with the type of heat that makes the air ring like glass. Thin, brittle, waiting for the smallest sound to shatter it. The sea shimmered like a lie told beautifully.

Tourists spilled along the headland in a bright, noisy pilgrimage: phones raised, hats askew, sunscreen gleaming like armour. They took photos of the lighthouse with the reverence of people who mistake distance for history.

I kept walking past them as if through a dream.

The bench was still mine, though I now had to share it with the world.

For weeks, the seam was silent.

The air, once doubled and humming, was only air again. Ordinary, polite, and deaf.

Still, I spoke into it anyway.

Sometimes aloud. Sometimes in pencil, on scraps of paper I left beneath the loose bolt with my small apostrophes to absence.

Are you safe?

Did they take the light apart yet?

The sea hasn't changed its voice, but I have.

I knew she might never read them, but hope is a habit, and habits are the bones of faith. So, I came each evening, thermos in hand, until the guard at the car park waved at me like a man humouring a ghost.

Then, in late January, after a week of windless days, the seam bloomed.

It began as a shimmer over the water, a faint second horizon, and then—there she was.

Her coat flapped around her ankles, hair wilder than I'd ever seen it. The light caught in it like gold trying to remember itself. My chest ached at the sight. I wanted to step through, to steady her, to feel again the weight of her reality against mine.

"You're back," I said, half a prayer, half disbelief.

"I never left," she said, smiling tiredly. "Time did."

Her voice wove through the air, soft but edged with fatigue, like a violin string tuned just past perfect. She told me the lighthouse had been refitted, the lenses replaced, the families moved inland.

"The world insists on marching forward," she said, "even when no one has asked it to."

Her voice wavered on forward, and I felt it in my ribs, that tender vibration of loss disguised as progress.

She looked older in that moment.

Not in face or form, but in the way weariness had taken residence behind her eyes. It suited her somehow.

The gravity of her time.

The beauty that doesn't ask to be noticed but demands reverence when you do.

We had only a few minutes before the seam began its quiet collapse, that familiar pulling back of the impossible. I talked fast, desperate to fill the dwindling air. I told her everything I'd said into the silence: about the tourists, again about my mother's passing, about my fear that history had swallowed her whole.

She listened, eyes bright, mouth still, the faintest crease at the corner of her lips betraying emotion held in good manners.

When I faltered, she whispered, "You've kept faith."

And because the distance between us suddenly felt intolerable, I reached toward her through the shimmer.

My fingers met the faint resistance of the seam—like warm glass, pliant, teasing.

She mirrored the gesture.

This time, the hum deepened, lower, more deliberate. The air thickened between us—heavy, trembling, charged.

For a moment it felt alive, as if it had blood and memory. Her palm hovered a breath from mine, the heat of her skin ghosting across the invisible boundary.

Neither of us moved.

The sound of the sea faded until all I could hear was the small, private thunder of my pulse. Her breath fogged the space between us, and it was almost enough to imagine warmth shared, lips meeting somewhere beyond permission.

"Eliza, I want you so much," I whispered, though the sound barely made it through my throat.

She smiled—a slow, knowing smile that curled at the edges. "Daniel. I do as well."

The way she said my name could have unstitched the sky.

When the seam finally folded, she didn't step back. The light bent around her, her outline dissolving as though she were made of breath and memory.

"I found your notes," she said as her voice blurred. "Every one of them."

"You read them?"

"I kept them," she said. "Even the ones the wind tried to steal."

And then she was gone.

The wind rushed in to fill her shape, the sound almost merciful. The air, still hot from her absence, pressed against me as if reluctant to forget.

I sat down on the bench, dizzy with the aftertaste of her presence. The world felt overexposed—too bright, too loud, too human.

I leaned forward, elbows on knees, and laughed once, quietly. "You never left," I murmured to the air. "But you keep arriving, anyway."

The sea answered in its unending grammar, all consonants, and insistence.

I stayed until night fell, tracing the memory of her warmth in the air, half expecting the seam to reopen, half afraid it might.

When I finally rose, the horizon was molten with afterglow. The light from the refitted lantern swept across the water, brighter now, but somehow lonelier.

At home, I couldn't sleep.

The heat clung to me, stubborn as thought. I closed my eyes and saw her again: her hair wild, her mouth forming my name, her hand reaching through the impossible as though desire itself could teach physics a new language.

For the first time in months, I let myself imagine not just seeing her again but feeling her. Skin against skin, century against century, the boundary forgotten.

I fell asleep to the hum of the ceiling fan, which, for just a moment, sounded like the seam remembering how to sing.

CHAPTER 14

SIGNALS IN THE DARK

Eliza

The world narrowed to lists. Lists of rations, of names, of messages to be encoded and sent. Lists of who had gone and who had not yet returned. Life itself had been alphabetised for efficiency. Men left; women took their places in kitchens, hospitals, and telegraph rooms, stitching the country together with Morse and prayer. Even the sea seemed busier, carrying troop ships instead of whales.

At night, the light still turned. I tended it with hands that had grown thinner but steadier, the rhythm of duty etched into my bones. The lantern no longer whispered to Daniel—it spoke of convoys and fog, of coded flashes and warnings. Yet on some nights, when the wind dropped to that note, we'd named our own, the seam flickered faintly, like a memory rehearsing itself. I would hold my breath, listening for him in the spaces between sound.

The first time it returned properly, I was exhausted. My apron smelled of oil and damp wool. My eyes burned from nights without sleep, translating telegrams until numbers became ghosts. I'd gone to the lantern simply to breathe where duty and loss met in the quietest compromise.

Then the air shifted. Doubled.

And once again, there he was.

My Daniel.

"You look tired," he said.

"War is an untidy thing," I replied, smiling faintly. "It gets into everything."

He looked stricken, as if guilt could cross the centuries and arrive intact. His expression made my heart ache and warm all at once.

"You know what happens, don't you?" he said quietly. "I mean, how does it end?"

I nodded. "I know enough."

"And still you—" He stopped, the rest caught in his throat, in the same way grief gets caught in time.

"I still love you," I finished for him.

His shoulders fell, a soundless sigh of relief and sorrow. "It's not fair," he said finally. "You're living through something I can only read about."

"Then read kindly," I said.

"History forgets softness first."

We spoke then in half-sentences and unfinished thoughts. We talked about hope as if it were contraband, rationed carefully, meant to be shared in small, deliberate portions. He told me that the world beyond mine had its own wars, invisible but just as cruel. I told him I'd been teaching the keeper's boy to use the lamp in code—spelling out names in flashes of light for ships that might never see them.

He smiled, the kind that breaks your heart by healing it. "That's what we're doing too," he said softly. "Flashes in the dark. Hoping someone understands."

The seam trembled then, threatening to break. I could feel it pulling at the air, eager to reclaim what it had given.

"Not yet," I whispered. "Please, not yet."

We held it steady with words.

We spoke nonsense and comfort and little fragments of memory — anything to keep the air taut with meaning. He described the colour of the sea in his world, greener, louder. I told him the fog had smelled of smoke from the training ships. He said my name like an anchor. I said his like a secret I meant to keep.

It lasted five minutes longer than it should have, which is the measure of faith.

When the seam finally gave in, it didn't snap or vanish— it sighed. The air folded itself neatly, almost tenderly, as if thanking us for our effort.

I stood a while after, the lamp's hum still in my ears, the ghost of his presence warming the chill between my palms. The world outside resumed its noise—waves, wind, distant orders—but none of it reached the quiet we'd made.

Later, in my journal, I wrote carefully: Love, even in wartime, finds new ways to signal.

Then, for the first time in weeks, I slept.

And in the dream that followed, the light turned by itself, and every sweep of its beam spelled a single word across the sea: I am alive.

CHAPTER 15

THE POSTCARD

Daniel

It was a Tuesday when I found the postcard.

Tuesdays aren't meant for miracles. They're for laundry and traffic lights that take too long. For being super productive at the office. For lukewarm coffee and the creeping suspicion that your best stories are already behind you. So, naturally, that was the day it happened.

The gift shop was the kind of place I usually avoided—too many keychains, too much forced cheer, the faint hum of a till where nostalgia was sold by the gram. But it was hot that afternoon, the heat that makes the world wobble slightly and the promise of air-conditioning was reason enough to wander in.

Inside, the place smelled like varnish, sunscreen, and someone's idea of the ocean bottled for profit. The shelves gleamed with mugs printed with cartoon seagulls, magnets shaped like lighthouses, and snow globes where glitter pretended to be sea spray. I was halfway to leaving when I saw it.

Tucked into a carousel between "Greetings from Camden" and a stack of novelty bookmarks shaped like pelicans—there it was:

1912 - Waratah Sands Lighthouse.

Sepia. Faded. The brown that remembers too much.

The lighthouse stood proud, the sea pretending docility around it. The headland was younger, rougher, its grasses still holding the wild arrogance of unphotographed land. The sky was pale and endless—the sort of colour the world wears when it hasn't yet decided on history.

I stood there staring like an idiot. My heart thudded. I think I actually grinned—the grin that makes people shift away slightly, in case madness is contagious.

The woman behind the counter looked up and smiled politely. "Good find," she said.

"Good?" I nearly laughed. "It's perfect."

She nodded, unaware that I was one breath away from proposing to a postcard.

I turned it over. Blank. No stamp, no handwriting, no message—just an open invitation to be claimed by someone foolish enough to believe that paper can hold miracles.

On impulse—because that's how these things always start—I bought it. Slid it into a paper bag with trembling fingers, paid in exact change, and left before I said something sentimental to the cash register. Back at the café, I ordered a flat white and sat outside, the postcard resting on the table like a living thing. I traced the edge.

1912.

Her year.

I could almost feel the hum beneath my fingertips, as if the air was rehearsing the seam again.

I didn't write on it. I couldn't. The silence between us had earned its dignity. But I did the next best thing—I mailed it to myself. Addressed, stamped, and sent, as though daring time to deliver proof.

Two days later, it arrived.

I stood in the kitchen staring at the envelope as if it might explode into light. When I slid it open and saw that sepia image again, I swear the room tilted a little. The sea, the tower, the small stretch of sky—it was all there, familiar and impossibly near.

I pinned it to the fridge beneath the WARATAH SANDS magnet, my own accidental shrine. The postcard stared back, composed and civil, the type of picture that belonged to a world before chaos. Too still. Too polite.

Eliza's world was never still. It was salt and wind and brass polished to defiance. It was motion. I whispered, "You wouldn't have stood still for this."

Still, I couldn't look away.

Later that week, I went back to the visitor centre. Maybe to feel near her. Maybe to see if lightning strikes twice.

Behind the counter stood a woman I hadn't seen before—sixties, hair like driftwood, eyes soft grey, the colour of the sea before rain. She had the sort of face that made you want to tell her things.

"Lovely day," I said, and instantly regretted the banality.

She smiled. "They usually are out here."

We fell into an easy conversation about the lighthouse, its restoration, the storms that nearly took it, the stories that refused to sink. I told her I'd always felt drawn to the place, that I came often. She nodded, her gaze patient, maybe amused.

"My grandmother worked here once," she said, wiping her hands on a tea towel. "Before she married and moved inland."

Something in me stilled. "Really? What was her name?"

She said it with no ceremony at all. "Eliza. Eliza Farrow."

The air left my lungs in a rush.

"She used to say," the woman went on, "that the sea talked back to her. Drove my grandfather mad. Said she'd come in with salt on her skin and stories in her eyes."

I almost laughed. My heart was hammering so hard I thought she'd hear it. "Maybe it did," I said softly.

"Hmm?"

"The sea," I managed. "Maybe it talked back."

She gave me a polite smile—the kind you give tourists who say too much—and rang up my postcard purchase without noticing I was standing in the centre of a revelation.

Before I left, she added, "Funny thing—she always kept a tin of barley sweets. Hated them herself but wouldn't be without them. Said they kept her company."

My throat closed. "She wasn't wrong."

She looked puzzled, but kind. "Would you like a bag?"

"No," I said, my voice too bright. "No, this is fine. Perfect, actually."

I think I almost skipped to the car. I grinned the entire drive home like a man who'd just stolen fire from the gods and gotten away with it.

That night, I climbed the headland with the postcard in my pocket. The heat had broken; the air was damp with promise. The sea shimmered with the pale silver of things about to be forgiven.

I poured two cups of tea as always, the steam curling like small ghosts. I raised mine to the empty air.

"Your granddaughter sells postcards," I said. "And she has your eyes."

The sea shushed me gently, as if embarrassed by my joy. Then, for just a moment, the air brightened—the faintest flicker, a breath caught between sigh and song.

I took it as an answer.

I laughed then, out loud, ridiculously and unashamed. "You see, Eliza? You've gone and multiplied. You're everywhere now."

The wind lifted, playful, carrying that faint, low hum I hadn't heard in months. It moved through me like a memory reborn.

Sometimes, faith isn't about waiting for miracles.

It's recognising them when they come disguised as ordinary days—a sepia postcard, a polite shopkeeper, a name spoken by chance that rewrites the sky.

That night, I pinned the postcard back on the fridge. It looked different now.

Alive, almost smug.

"Don't look at me like that," I told it. "You started this."

I made tea and stood by the window until the beam of the lighthouse swung across the water, silver and sure.

And I swore I heard her laugh in it.

Low, familiar, mischievous like a promise remembering itself.

CHAPTER 16

A PINCH OF FOREVER

Eliza

By late winter, I had measured time by the light's moods rather than by calendars. The almanac still hung by the door, its pages curling at the edges, but it might as well have been a relic. The light was my clock, the sea my hourglass. Each morning, I read their temperaments: calm, sullen, exuberant, petulant.

The war rumbled like a storm too far off to demand obedience. Its thunder reached us only in telegrams and ration schedules, in the clipped voices of officials who seemed faintly annoyed that the horizon refused to salute. Here on the headland, the rhythms of tide and lamp kept their own peace.

Then, one quiet evening, the air changed key—the old note, our note.

I left the kitchen mid-sentence, the kettle still boiling, and nearly tripped over Mrs. Barker's kitten, who had claimed the bread basket as a fort. My apron smelled of fish stew and frustration, but I didn't care. The seam was calling.

By the time I reached the cliff path, the sea had turned to pewter, smooth and deliberate. The horizon had doubled. And there he was—Daniel—exactly where he had always been, coat collar turned up, waiting.

"It's been months," he said, relief roughening his voice.

"It has," I whispered. "But the sea doesn't forget its tune."

The seam widened more than it ever had before, trembling like a curtain held by two invisible hands. The air softened; light spilled between us like a secret finally told. And then—for the second time in our impossible history—we were in the same room.

Not for long. No miracle ever lasts longer than a breath. But long enough for the body to remember what the heart already knows.

His hand found mine, warm and steady. The skin of time felt fragile under our touch, thin as a soap bubble, but it held. His thumb traced the back of my knuckles, and I could feel the century between us sigh.

We didn't speak at first. Some silences are too full to interrupt. Then we filled the air with everything we'd hoarded for this impossible moment—small things, ordinary things, the kind you never realise you've missed until you can say them aloud.

I told him about Mrs Barker's new kitten, which had claimed the keeper's hat as a bed and hissed at anyone who dared to correct it. He told me of a city-wide power outage— how, for one strange night, the stars returned to the people, and everyone stopped scrolling through their glowing boxes long enough to look up.

He watched me while he spoke, eyes bright with that mix of wonder and affection that makes you feel both infinite and embarrassingly visible.

"Do you know what I miss?" he said. "Cooking for someone."

I made a face. "Oh, I burn everything. Bread, stews, optimism. But I'd burn it gladly for you."

He grinned. "You? You? The woman who measures light like a clockmaker and lectures the wind about precision. I don't believe you could burn anything."

"You've never met my porridge," I said. "It's a war crime in three acts."

He laughed, rich and full, and the sound startled the seam into another few minutes of generosity.

"Tell me what you'd cook," I challenged.

He pretended to think deeply, stroking his chin. "Two eggs and hope."

"Hope's scarce," I replied. "You'd better whisk carefully."

"Fine," he said. "Then a spoonful of daring."

I grinned. "And a dash of forgiveness."

He nodded solemnly. "Served warm."

We laughed until our ribs hurt—an unseemly, undignified laughter that crossed time without asking permission. It was glorious.

When we calmed, I told him how I'd learned to stretch flour with mashed potatoes, how Mrs. Barker swore by dripping for everything, and how the keeper's boy had once mistaken salt for sugar and nearly ruined an entire batch of scones.

He chuckled. "You'd hate my era's cooking shows. They turn recipes into competitions."

"Competitions?" I gasped. "Cooking is a courtship, not a duel!"

He laughed so hard he had to wipe his eyes. "Remind me never to cross you in a kitchen."

"Don't worry," I said. "You'd be too busy being overfed."

"By you?"

"By me," I said proudly. "Burnt offerings and all."

When the seam thinned again, we didn't panic. We simply leaned closer, as though proximity could bend the rulebook. The air shivered between us, restless but tender.

"Until next we're borrowed," I told him.

He nodded, his eyes holding mine as if the act itself could anchor him. "Until next time."

The seam pulsed once, a heartbeat shared between centuries, and folded shut.

I stood there in the soft dark, feeling the echo of his warmth on my skin, the ghost of laughter still trapped in the air. The wind carried the smell of the stew I'd abandoned earlier; it was almost certainly burning.

"Well," I told the night, "that's dinner ruined again. And worth every bite."

Mrs Barker scolded me later for "wasting good broth on romance," but I only smiled. Because some loves don't require tears—they require endurance, and occasionally, a second kettle.

That night I rewrote one of my recipes in the margin of my journal:

For one impossible meeting:
1 storm waiting its turn
2 hearts impatient with physics
A pinch of faith
Stir until the air changes key

And for once, I slept with the smell of burnt stew and happiness in the same room.

CHAPTER 17

THE LAST NOTE OF THE WIND

Daniel

The weeks that followed were heavy with silence.

You know. The type of silence that doesn't sit still.

It breathes, hums, presses itself into the fabric of your days until you mistake it for company.

I went through the daily motions: work, bills, watched Netflix but did not pay attention, groceries, half-listened to conversations about the weather.

Everything carried on with its mindless continuity, as if the world were a machine that refused to notice the piece it had misplaced.

Yet underneath all that ordinary noise, I could feel it.

The faint vibration of the seam.

Not audible, not even tangible, just there.

Like a half-remembered melody waiting for the right breath to bring it back. The air sometimes trembled when I walked the headland, subtle as a heartbeat in the wrong place.

I stopped telling friends about my "evening walks." They smiled too kindly when I spoke of them. The smiles reserved for the well-intentioned unwell ready for the padded walls.

Good for you, Daniel, they'd say; fresh air helps.

And maybe it did, though it wasn't air I was looking for.

I let the subject die.

I became once more the man in the long coat standing by the sea for reasons that belonged to no one else.

Then came May.

The wind that night had a purpose.

It rose to a pitch that rattled the metal railings along the path, the sound like a thousand spoons in an empty sink or me dropping a hot casserole dish when I forgot to wear the padded heat-resistant gloves.

The sky was an anvil of clouds.

Black, heavy, waiting for lightning to strike some sense into it. I could smell rain, but threaded through it was something older, something that made the hair along my arms lift in quiet recognition.

Ozone, yes. But also, memory.

I felt the seam was nearby.

I could feel it before I saw it: that subtle doubling of the air, the way the world seemed to inhale and forget how to exhale. The air shimmered, hesitant, like an instrument long overdue for tuning.

And then it opened.

The sound wasn't grand.

It was small and deliberate.

It sounded like the sound of an old piano finally being played again. The shimmer pulsed faintly; the air quivering around its edges. I thought of Eliza's hands steadying the lantern, of her voice, patient and amused, saying, listen.

"Are you there?" I asked, my voice nearly lost to the roar.

The sea answered first, with a crash of water against stone.

I waited, my coat whipping against my legs, rain beginning to prick the air.

I waited until the waiting hurt.

Then, faintly, I heard her.

"I am here, my love," she said. "But only just."

Her voice drifted through the wind, thin and luminous, the way light seeps under a closed door.

The shimmer of her shape flickered in and out, half-light, half-wind, her face there, then gone.

"It's failing," she said.

"I know," I whispered.

"I'm not afraid," she added, and smiled.

Oh, that smile.

That beautiful, wonderful smile.

The one that always steadied me, the one that made every impossible thing feel like a decision rather than a miracle. "It was a gift to have this at all."

I wanted to protest.

To rage.

To demand that time explain itself, that the architecture of the universe stop building bridges only to watch them collapse.

"Why can't I have it forever?" I thought to myself.

But her calmness reached across the seam like a tide. It disarmed me.

"You taught me to look for the wind's key," I said. "I'll keep listening."

"And I'll keep the lamp trimmed," she answered. "Someone must keep it lit."

The wind softened briefly, almost respectfully.

The seam pulsed once, bright and thin, like a filament burning its last light.

Then it went dark.

The world exhaled.

I stood there for a long time; the rain turning everything silver. The sea calmed by degrees, like something pacified. I sat down on the bench, soaked through, and stayed until dawn.

The first gulls rose on the wind like scraps of light.

The sun made a slow, cautious entrance. I pulled out my pocketknife, a small, clumsy act of rebellion, and carved into the underside of the bench: D & E.

Crossed by a thin line, like the seam itself.

A mark no tourist would notice, but one the sea would remember.

When it was done, I leaned back, the wood damp against my spine, and let the morning wind dry my face.

"I told you," I whispered to the sea.

"Endurance is a skill, not a miracle."

And for the first time since she'd spoken, I swore I heard an answer, not in words, but in the tide's shift, in the rhythm of waves folding back into themselves. It sounded like someone agreeing softly and then turning up the lamp.

CHAPTER 18

INSTRUCTIONS FOR GENTLENESS

Eliza

The war pressed closer. Every morning now began with the hiss of ration tins opening, the soft thud of boots on the pier, and the murmured counting of numbers that always ended too soon. Faces in the village still smiled, but only with half their hearts; the rest had already gone—to the front, to the sea, to some unknowable ledger of loss.

Telegram boys rode through with their caps low, their bicycles whispering doom on oiled chains. Mrs. Barker stopped baking altogether; flour was rationed, and hope had to be saved for other recipes. Even the wind seemed thinner, its song more urgent.

Yet the lighthouse kept turning.

It had become, somehow, both my confessor and my accomplice. It listened to the world's noise and distilled it into light—one clean sweep after another, as though erasing chaos with rhythm. Even when the orders came to shutter it during convoy nights, I disobeyed. The world could go dark by command, but duty to love was harder to extinguish.

So, the lamp stayed lit, even when fear made the air tremble. I trimmed the wick, checked the oil, and whispered Daniel's name to the flame as if it could carry sound across centuries.

Then, one evening, the seam returned.

Not boldly—no, it came shyly, like a guest who's forgotten whether they're still welcome. The air flickered, hesitant but loyal, and I could feel the familiar soft pull of the impossible. His voice reached me first, stretched thin by distance but unmistakable.

"Eliza," he said. "You're still keeping the light."

"Someone must," I replied. "Otherwise, the sea will start telling its own stories again, and they're never flattering."

He laughed—blessed, grounding laughter. The kind that reminded me of life beyond telegrams and duty.

"I saw her again," he blurted, his tone gentling.

"Who?"

"Your granddaughter."

The word landed in my chest like an answered prayer. "You went back?"

He nodded, though the shimmer made his outline waver. "I told myself it was to buy more postcards, but truthfully, I just wanted to see her. To see you in her."

"And did you?" I asked, smiling despite myself.

"Yes," he said. "The same tilt of the head when you're pretending not to laugh. The same way of looking at the world like it owes you an answer but you'll forgive it if it tries hard enough. She sells fridge magnets now—tiny lighthouses that light up when you tap them. She said she liked to think they keep watch, even when no one's looking."

I covered my mouth to keep from crying. "That's her, then. My blood learning to love light."

"She told me her grandmother—you—used to hum while cooking," he added teasingly. "Said it was the only way you could trick the soup into tasting better."

I groaned. "Oh, I see the Farrow family has kept its tradition of slander alive and well."

He grinned. "So, it's true?"

I sighed dramatically. "Daniel, my cooking could defeat armies. My bread once killed a spoon."

He laughed so hard the shimmer flickered, and I felt the air strain with joy.

"Still," he said, catching his breath, "I like to think your stew could save a life or two. The way you tell stories about food makes me hungry even when I'm full."

"You're a terrible flatterer," I said, blushing despite the distance.

"And you," he said, "are a terrible liar. You know perfectly well you like it."

I did. I liked everything about him—the way he softened the edges of time, the way his words made the present less cruel.

When the laughter faded, he grew quieter, thoughtful. "Eliza, the seam feels weaker. Like it's forgetting how to hold itself open."

"I've felt it too," I said. "The air takes longer to change key."

He nodded. "Maybe... maybe we can leave something that remembers us, even if the air forgets."

"What do you mean?"

"Legacy," he said, his voice finding steadiness again. "Instructions for gentleness. If someone finds them—your notes, my journals—they'll know we existed. They'll know that even time can be kind sometimes."

I smiled through tears. "For the kind stranger who is us."

He looked startled, then delighted. "That's perfect."

So, we planned.

I promised to write another note, longer this time, describing our meetings and how the world itself had bent for us. He promised to keep a journal disguised as a tide record, hidden in plain sight among his world's ordinary archives.

When the seam dimmed, we hurried our words like two scribes at the end of a story.

"Eliza," he said, "if the world forgets us—"

"It won't," I interrupted. "We've made it into its air."

He closed his eyes. "I'll keep listening for the wind's key."

"And I'll keep the lamp trimmed," I said. "Someone must keep it lit."

The seam pulsed once, approving, like a heartbeat of light—and then it folded, slow and tender, into nothing.

That night, I wrote until my fingers cramped.

If love lives anywhere, it lives in instructions for gentleness.

If you find this, be kind to whatever you cannot understand.

We were two travellers, somewhere in time, and we found each other.

When I finished, I sealed it with wax and placed it beside the tin of barley sweets, our old reliquary of hope.

Outside, the wind had quieted to a whisper, the kind that belongs only to lovers and fools.

I imagined Daniel on his side, pen moving across paper at the same moment, his handwriting looping into mine through the seam of belief.

And for one soft instant, I swear I could see him—the tilt of his head, the furrow between his brows, the gentle concentration of a man writing something that mattered.

"Good night, my love," I said into the lamp's glow. "The world's still listening."

And the light turned once more, slow and steady, like a promise that refuses to fade.

CHAPTER 19

THE LAST NIGHT

Daniel

The night the seam returned it was remarkable at first.

The sea was calm, the waves were dark as ink, the ripples smaller than usual, its rhythm the steady breathing of something vast and patient. The air felt thick with moisty salt and the cicadas were exceptionally loud as well this evening. I felt the moist and faint scrape of the tall grass along the railings. The lighthouse beam moved in its slow, deliberate arc—steady, impartial, as though eternity had clocked in for another shift.

It felt too ordinary for a miracle, and maybe that's how all miracles arrive—wearing the quiet face of routine.

Then—the horizon doubled.

A shimmer spread across the water, thin as breath on glass, hesitant as if deciding whether the world deserved it again. I froze mid-step, afraid that even breathing might scare it off. My heart forgot its discipline and bolted into my throat.

And there—through the quivering light—stood Eliza.

Her silhouette gathered itself from the shimmer like a memory taking form. She stood straight against the wind, hair pinned up, coat fastened at the throat. Her face—older, yes, but radiant, certain. It was as if time itself had stepped aside to let her through.

"Daniel," she whispered, her voice threading perfectly through the seam.

"I'm here."

The air between us trembled once, then softened as if the universe, after all its rules and revisions, had made an exception.

The seam opened quietly and decisively, like a door that had been waiting too long for a knock.

And then—impossibly—we were in the same world.

Her hand rose first. Mine followed. The space between us disappeared. Her palm met mine—warm, human, whole.

Every part of me woke. Every nerve sang its own small hymn.

Her breath reached me before her words did, carrying the faint, familiar scent of lamp oil and lavender. I felt the tremor of her fingers as they traced the edge of my sleeve, then my wrist, as if confirming that the stories she'd written in the margins of her life had been real all along.

Her other hand slid up to my shoulder; I drew her closer, and the movement felt both foreign and inevitable.

We kissed—first gently, in disbelief, and then with the hunger of two souls trying to commit themselves to memory through touch.

Her lips were cool from the wind, warm beneath. The shock of it—how alive it felt—stole my breath. The world seemed to contract to the space between our mouths, where everything we'd ever said found a new translation.

When we parted, she rested her forehead against mine, her breath shaking, laughter and tears woven together. "I dreamt of this," she said.

"I didn't," I murmured, still dizzy. "I was afraid to make it smaller than this."

Her laugh turned into a soft, unguarded sigh, the sound of joy brushing up against disbelief. I felt it on my skin.

We stood like that for a long time, our hands wandering to relearn what eyes alone had loved—her jawline, the hollow beneath her throat, the line of her back beneath the wool of her coat. Each touch was reverent, exploratory, like reading braille from the heart's archive.

Her eyes lifted to mine—those steadfast eyes that always looked at the world as though it could be reasoned with—and she smiled, a little tremor of light passing through her.

"I used to wonder," she said softly, "what it would feel like—the world folding itself just long enough for us to fit inside it."

"And?" I asked, my voice catching.

"It feels," she said, "like forgiveness."

We kissed again, slower this time. Less hunger now, more promise. It was not passion but peace—an anchoring of one heartbeat to another. Around us, the air thickened with light, not bright but deep, as though the seam itself had learned how to breathe.

I cupped her face, tracing the small lines at the corners of her mouth—proof that she had lived, that time had tried and failed to make her less radiant.

When the seam tightened, we felt it together: the faint pull, the ache of farewell creeping back into the air.

She reached up and touched my cheek, her thumb brushing the corner of my mouth. Her hand trembled—not from fear, but from love steadying itself for goodbye.

"Don't be sad," she whispered. "We were never promised forever."

"I'd have settled for thirty seconds," I said, and she laughed—bright, unguarded, the sound of someone too alive to mourn.

Then the light folded.

The world snapped shut, quick as breath. The shimmer retreated; her voice dissolved into echo.

I stood on the headland alone, my palm still warm, the taste of salt and farewell mingling in the dark.

For a while, I couldn't move. The sea continued its endless rehearsal, whispering what it had always known: that nothing we love is ever truly gone—it simply learns another language.

I sat until the tide came in. The moon rose; a pale coin tossed into eternity.

And I realised she'd been right all along.

Nothing ends. It only changes rooms.

I leaned back, looking up at the slow, faithful spin of stars. "I'll see you in the wind's key," I whispered.

And the breeze, gentle and almost shy, shifted pitch— one note higher, as if answering.

Always.

CHAPTER 20

THE KEEPER OF THE SECOND LIGHT

Daniel

Years turn quietly when you stop measuring them by miracles. It's been decades since that last night on the headland.

Since the seam, the shimmer, the eight borrowed minutes that stitched two centuries together. I've lived whole seasons since then, maybe whole lives, yet sometimes I wake with the feeling that she's only just stepped into the next room.

Eliza Farrow.

Her name still moves through my mind like a melody I once knew the words to but now hum instead.

The lighthouse stands differently now, taller somehow, though its bones are the same. The keeper's cottage was restored, painted in colours the sea tolerates. The museum boards out front speak of "dedicated service," "wartime duty," "heroic illumination." None mentions what the light truly kept—the space between time and love, the proof that the world sometimes folds its rules for kindness.

The gift shop sits where the signal room used to be. Glass shelves, postcards, polished driftwood carved into anchors. It smells faintly of salt and varnish, as if the place refuses to forget its ancestry.

And behind the counter there's always her granddaughter.

Sarah Farrow.

The first time I met her properly was years ago, when the world still printed postcards in glossy colour. I told myself I'd only stopped by to see the new restoration, but my heart was already rehearsing disbelief.

She looked up from arranging trinkets, smiled, and in that single moment I saw Eliza, tilted head, calm certainty, eyes that seemed to see through history instead of around it.

"Back again?" she asked. "You've come often."

"Habit," I said. "Old habits are the hardest to break."

She laughed.

"I know. My grandmother used to say that about the sea."

We talked as we always do.

At first, about ordinary things.

Souvenir stock, visitor numbers, the stubbornness of coastal weather.

But she had a way of listening that made everything feel like a confession. When I mentioned her grandmother had once spoken of the wind as if it had moods, Sarah's expression softened.

"Yes," she said. "She wrote that once; in a note they found hidden behind a shelf when the lighthouse was refitted. I keep a copy here."

She pulled it from a drawer: a piece of aged paper, the writing delicate and slanted. I knew the words before I read them.

If love lives anywhere, it lives in instructions for gentleness.

If you find this, be kind to whatever you cannot understand.

I swallowed hard and the world tilted.

She was looking at me with quiet curiosity, unaware that she had just handed me back the proof of everything I had ever believed.

"She must've been extraordinary," I said softly.

Sarah smiled.

"She was. My mother said she had the patience of a saint and the temper of a sailor."

"She was more than that," I murmured, before I could stop myself.

Sarah tilted her head again, exactly the way Eliza used to, and for a heartbeat the air felt doubled.

Then a customer walked in, and the moment folded neatly away.

Years passed.

Sarah took over the shop entirely when her mother fell ill. She modernised it. Turned it into something warm and bright, full of local art and stories.

And she made a new sign: The Keeper's Gift.

Every summer, she adds a new display.

Letters, fragments of history, maritime relics. Last year, she placed the tin of barley sweets behind glass, the one they'd found with Eliza's note. Visitors walk by, smile, and read the inscription without knowing that the ink once crossed a seam in time.

I visit once or twice a year now, sometimes more.

She always has tea ready.

We talk about tides and tourists, the usual poetry of coastal living.

I tell her stories about the lighthouse in its "quieter" years, and she laughs, saying I sound like I lived there.

I suppose in a way I did.

After Eliza, I married.

Her name was Margaret.

A kind, grounding soul who could make an argument sound like a hymn. We built a life steady as brickwork. Two children, both grown now: a son who designs harbours, a daughter who teaches literature and loves the sea without knowing why.

I never told them about Eliza.

Not because it was a secret, but because it was something better.

An understanding too large for explanation.

Margaret and I shared fifty years.

When she died, I scattered her ashes near the southern rocks, where the waves never quite rest. Grief came differently that time. Quieter, less like drowning, more like the tide withdrawing politely.

In the evenings, I still walk to the headland.

The bench is gone now, replaced by one of those stainless-steel memorial seats with names etched into plaques. I carved D + E beneath the old one, years ago, but I never went looking to see if it survived.

Some things are best left unconfirmed.

Sarah once asked me why I always visit near sunset.

I told her the truth—that it's when the wind changes key.

She laughed, but kindly, and said, "Then I'll keep the door open, in case it carries her in."

She does too.

Every night before closing, she props the shop door with a piece of coral and says, "For luck."

Sometimes when I stand on the headland, the air does something familiar. It trembles faintly, as if trying to hum a forgotten tune.

It never opens.

It doesn't need to.

I've learned that presence isn't always about proximity. Sometimes it's the faith that what was still is, somewhere just beyond sight.

The lighthouse beam turns above me with the same patient rhythm. Below it, Sarah's window glows warm in the dark. I imagine Eliza watching through my eyes, proud of this descendant who still tends the light, who keeps her laughter in circulation.

Before I leave, I always whisper the same thing: "She's doing well. You'd like her."

The sea listens, as it always does.

And every so often, when the air grows still, I hear it. The wind shifted key, just once.

It sounds like a door opening somewhere between worlds.

And I smile, because after all these years, I finally understand what Eliza meant: Nothing ends.

It only changes rooms.

CHAPTER 21

FINAL LETTER

Daniel

My Dearest Eliza,

It's late. The house is quiet, and the wind has begun its gentle song against the windows—the one you taught me to listen for. The world has grown smaller around me, as worlds do when the body forgets what the heart still remembers. My children visit, my grandchildren too, filling these rooms with laughter that feels borrowed from another life. And yet, every evening when the light fades, my thoughts travel to Waratah Sands, where the sea keeps our story.

I am an old man now. My hands tremble when I write, but I find comfort in the movement of pen to paper. You once said that writing was how we remind time that we were here. Perhaps that's what this is—a reminder.

I saw her today—your granddaughter, Sarah. She's older now, though she carries it beautifully, the way you did. She owns the gift shop completely; she runs it with the same quiet precision you gave to the lantern. The shelves gleam, the glass cases are polished, and she always keeps a candle burning near the old tin of barley sweets. She says it's for luck, but I know it's a vigil.

Sometimes she tells visitors, "My grandmother worked here when this place was still bone and wind." She doesn't know I was once the man who waited at the edge of that wind, but she looks at me kindly, as if some part of her does.

I have lived a good life, Eliza. Margaret—my wife, my patient friend—gave me years of peace. Our children gave me reason. They never knew about the seam, about you. How could they? The world has its laws, and miracles rarely survive the courtroom of reason. But every now and then, when my daughter walks by the sea, she hums a tune I've never taught her. And my son, who studies the tides, keeps a small journal of the wind's behaviour. I like to believe that what we loved has threaded itself through them, quiet as breath.

You once wrote, If love lives anywhere, it lives in instructions for gentleness. I think I understand that now. Gentleness is how we endure what the world refuses to explain.

There were times after you were gone that I felt you near. In the hush before dawn. In the way fog rolls in from the sea and hesitates before touching land. Once during a storm, I swore I saw the horizon double again, faint but certain. I didn't chase it. I whispered only, "Thank you."

Sarah tells me she's thinking of expanding the shop—adding a small tea corner, where visitors can sit and watch the light turn. "The Keeper's Table," she plans to call it. She asked what I thought of the name. I told her it was perfect.

When she wasn't looking, I slipped something under the old display of letters. My last entry, sealed in wax. It reads simply:

We kept the light on.

It was enough.

If anyone ever finds it, he / she / they'll think it belongs to a keeper or a sailor. And they'll be right, in their way.

The sea outside is loud tonight—restless, familiar. It sounds like you when you were trying not to laugh. I like to imagine that somewhere, the seam is open again, just for a heartbeat, and that you are standing at the railing, lamp trimmed, watching over everything we've made.

I'll be joining you soon, love. Don't come too quickly. Let me arrive the way the tide does—quiet, deliberate, inevitable. And when I do, I'll bring tea, and we'll sit again on that impossible bench between worlds. You can tell me all the things the sea's been saying, and I'll finally understand the words.

Until then, I'll keep listening for the wind's key.

Yours, always,
Daniel

When Daniel's great-grandchildren found his journal years later, the ink on that last line had smudged, as if touched by rain or perhaps by someone's hand reaching through time to steady his words.

And that night, as if obeying an ancient promise, the wind changed key once more.

ABOUT THE AUTHOR

José F. Nodar is an Australian Cuban author, reviewer, and literary entrepreneur based in Spring Farm, NSW. He is the founder of Quick Story Tales Online and World Book Reviews, initiatives supporting and promoting both emerging and established authors worldwide.

José's writing blends humour, sentiment, and quiet realism, often drawing from the landscapes and community spirit of regional New South Wales. His fiction, including Whispers from My Wife, The Northport Coffee Group, and Stories to Share with My Partner Collection, explores universal themes of love, loss, and rediscovery.

When not writing, José can be found reading at a local café, walking along Spring Farm's footpaths, or championing local authors and creative groups through interviews and newsletters.

Please visit https://worldbookreviews.com.au/ and let me know what you thought of this book of short stories and poetry.

Good, bad, or indifferent, I will always welcome your honest opinion.

Send me an email at info@jfnodar.com.au

Thank you for your purchase!

Other books by José F. Nodar:

Novels in English

The Danny Monk Trilogy

Books, Pens & Larceny
Mending Hearts at Crystal Cove
A Love Finally Spoken

The Mallard E. Benson Trilogy

The Girl Who Didn't Come Home
The Ones That Got Away
The Ghost We Owe

Mystery

The Ghost Detective's First Case
The Northport Coffee Group

Romance

The Teacher's Assistant
A Night of Love
Maybe This Is Everything
Love in Stereo

Somewhere In Time

When Love Remembers

Science Fiction & Fantasy

The Compass Legacy
The Universe Between Us
The Time Bus
The Last Light of Aurethis

Children

The Hamster Who Whispered Back

Humour

SEX

Anthologies of Stories and Poetry

Quick Stories & Poems Volume I
Quick Stories & Poems Volume 2
Quick Stories & Poems Volume 3

Collections of Stories and Poetry

Stories to Share with My Partner Book 1
Stories to Share with My Partner Book 2
Stories to Share with My Partner Book 3
Stories to Share with My Partner Book 4
Stories to Share with My Partner Book 5
Stories to Share with My Partner Book 6
Stories to Share with My Partner Book 7
Stories to Share with My Partner Book 8
Stories to Share with My Partner Book 9
Stories to Share with My Partner Book 10
Stories to Share with My Partner Book 11
Stories to Share with My Partner Book 12

Libros en Español
La Trilogía de Danny Monk

Un Amor Expresado
Reparando Corazones en Crystal Cove
Un Amor Finalmente Declarado

Colecciones de Cuentos y Poemas

Cuentos Para Compartir con Mi Pareja Libro 1
Cuentos Para Compartir con Mi Pareja Libro 2
Cuentos Para Compartir con Mi Pareja Libro 3

Ciencia Ficción y Fantasía

Somewhere In Time

El Autobús del Tiempo